THE SOUND OF HIS VOICE

---⁂---

Rebecca Bricker

Folio&Leaf

The Sound of His Voice

Copyright © Rebecca Bricker, 2017.
All rights reserved.

ISBN-13: 9780998277004
ISBN-10: 0998277002

Folio & Leaf Publishing
USA

Cover image created by Philip Samuel Sundqvist and Julio Nicacio
from Pierre Bonnard's *Nu dans un intérieur*

Cover graphic design by Elizabeth MacFarland

Without limiting the rights under the copyright reserved above, no part of this publication may be reproduced, stored in a retrieval system, or transmitted in any form or by any means (electronic, mechanical, photocopying, recording, web posting or otherwise), without the prior written permission of the Author.

*To the man whose luggage cart locked wheels with mine
at Charles de Gaulle Airport*

and to Marthe and Renée

ALSO BY REBECCA BRICKER

Tales from Tavanti:
An American Woman's Mid-Life Adventure in Italy

Not a True Story

The Secret of Marie

Pierre Bonnard
(1867 - 1947)

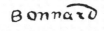

Paris ~ July 2015

LIZ

THE WINDOWS OF Charles de Gaulle's Terminal 2 streamed with rain. Everyone around me seemed to be dressed for winter, even though it was July 2. I was dressed for my hopefully sunny destination, wearing a colorful tropical skirt and a white linen blouse. I looked like I had just arrived from Hawaii and everyone else had come in from Siberia. I was feeling rather conspicuous as I pushed my cart toward the TGV railway station at the far end of the terminal.

I got tangled in a crush of tourists and suitcases and the wheels of my luggage cart locked with another. The handsome guy attached to the cart smiled at me. He wiggled our wheels apart.

"Do you happen to know where the Sheraton is?" he asked.

"I think it's this way." I pointed in the direction we were heading.

"Where did you fly in from?" he asked. I think the tropical skirt had caught his eye.

"Los Angeles. What about you?"

"New York. Are you staying in Paris?"

"No. I'm catching a train to Provence."

"When?"

"Noon."

He glanced at his watch. "Would you like to have coffee?"

Plenty of time, I thought. "That would be nice."

He smiled. "My name is Kamal, by the way." He had lovely hazel eyes.

"I'm Liz."

We wheeled our carts into the Sheraton lobby, where we were stopped by the bellman. "You must leave your carts here with me," he told us politely.

Kamal explained to him that he was checking in and would like his bags taken to his room. I explained to him that I wasn't checking in and would need to retrieve my bags shortly. The bellman nodded as if he understood us.

I sank into a plush sofa in the lounge by the lobby, suddenly feeling my jet lag, as Kamal checked in at reception. I wondered what his story was. I would find out soon enough, but I tried to fill in the blanks in advance. I guessed he was about my age, mid-30s. He had a British accent, with a slight Indian lilt. He was casually dressed in jeans, a light-blue shirt and a suede jacket the color of tobacco. He had a nice build, dark wavy hair...and those lovely hazel eyes.

In a few minutes, he joined me on the sofa. We ordered coffee. I saw his wedding ring at the same moment he noticed I had no wedding ring.

Kamal was from Mumbai, but lived in London. His business travels took him around the world, quite literally on this trip: China, Toronto, New York and now Paris. He owned an import-export company.

Kamal had a four-year-old son named Yamir. He proudly showed me a photo on his phone. Yamir was adorable.

"He has your eyes," I said.

Kamal took me in. "What about you? Are you married?"

"I'm divorced. No kids." I could tell Kamal was very interested in filling in the blanks about me.

"What's taking you to Provence?"

"A holiday. I'm starting a big project here in Paris in a couple of weeks."

"You'll be in Paris? For how long?"

"A month or two, maybe longer."

"What do you do?"

"I'm an art-forgery specialist."

"Seriously? What are you working on?"

"A painting by Pierre Bonnard was auctioned in London recently for a lot of money. The new owner now believes the painting is a fake and is suing Sotheby's, who has hired me to do an evaluation."

"So you're like an art detective."

"Sort of."

"Where will you be staying here?"

"I haven't seen the apartment yet. It's somewhere in Saint-Germain-des-Prés. Not far from the Musée d'Orsay, which will be convenient."

"You'll be working at the museum?"

"I'll have an office there."

Kamal was intrigued. "So where's home?"

"L.A. mostly. My parents are in D.C. I travel a lot with my work. I'm a bit rootless, actually."

"How long have you been divorced – if you don't mind me asking."

"Two years."

I could tell he wanted to explore that subject. But instead, he picked up the menu on the coffee table in front of us. "Shall we order something? You must be hungry. When was your last real meal?"

I laughed. "I'm not sure. A bagel at LAX comes to mind."

"What would you like?" He slid closer to me on the sofa. I could smell his cologne, laced with exotic notes I couldn't name.

We ordered omelets and croissants and more coffee. We decided not to move to a table. My legs felt rubbery. I didn't want to leave our cushy seats.

Our conversation wandered aimlessly and easily. We shared the same joy of wanderlust. Our paths had crisscrossed many times in our travels. How nice to randomly lock wheels with a kindred spirit, I thought.

As the waiter took away our empty plates, I suddenly longed for a nap. I slid deeper into the cushion and laid my head back. In my very relaxed state, I wasn't ready for what came next.

"Let's spend the afternoon together," Kamal said. "Can you take a later train?"

"What about your meeting?"

"It can wait. I want to spend the day with you."

We looked at each other in a freeze-frame moment, when what-ifs loom large. I saw a little boy named Yamir with hazel eyes – and imagined the wife who was waiting in London.

"I really need to make that train." I looked at my watch and sat bolt upright. "My god, is it really 11:30?"

I'm sure Kamal knew I wanted to say yes to him. And Fate, it would seem, was on his side. When we went to the lobby to retrieve my bags, the bellman looked blankly at us. "I took all the bags to your room, sir."

I looked nervously at my watch. My train was leaving in 25 minutes. Suddenly, my armpits felt damp.

Kamal turned to me. "I'll get your bags. Would you like to come upstairs and freshen up?"

Another freeze-frame moment. My armpits were spewing.

"I'll wait here," I said calmly. But apparently, I didn't look calm.

"I'll hurry."

I sat down on a firm chair in the lobby. One word kept running through my mind: shit, shit, shit, shit, shit.

Five minutes went by. I stared at the elevator doors, willing them to open. Another five minutes. *Shit, shit, shit.*

I contemplated my situation. My luggage was in the room of a man I hardly knew. Whether I made my train depended wholly on his honor and the efficiency of the Sheraton's elevators. *SHIT!*

An elevator door opened, revealing the human equivalent of a bucket of anchovies. Kamal tumbled out with my bags, looking as panicked as I felt.

We quickly hugged and said good-bye.

"Where can I reach you?" he asked.

I handed him my card and impulsively kissed him on the cheek. And then I ran for the train.

I boarded with a few minutes to spare. All the way to Avignon, I dozed with the scent of Kamal's cologne on my blouse and wondered about WHAT IF.

KAMAL

Our wedding night was awkward. No, it was awful.

It was no surprise really. Our time alone together before our marriage could be counted in minutes, maybe a few hours total. Hard to believe in the modern age.

Her father went to school with mine in Mumbai – Bombay, then. They played cricket together. Our mothers were best friends, too. It was a neat package. Our lives were planned for us from the day Aja was born, three years after I came into a well-ordered world bearing the vestiges of British colonial rule. Our destiny was quietly presented to us on a silver tray from my mother's tea service or hers.

I grew up with Aja ever present. But I always thought I'd have a say in the end. She was a sweet girl. Very shy. A loving, obedient daughter. She excelled in school and went away to university. I remember thinking at the time, when she left Mumbai, that I finally had some breathing room. I went to London to study economics. I had a healthy libido and didn't hesitate to keep my bed warm with a variety of young beauties. I fell for one of them, an English-rose-of-a-woman with long dark hair that smelled of her jasmine shampoo. I feasted on her plump breasts, daily. Sex with her was wonderful. Sometimes, I still dream of her.

Aja barely let me near her on our wedding night. I wanted to be a loving husband. She was a virgin, of course. I understood her anxiety.

She looked ravishing as she entered the bedroom from the dressing area, wearing a diaphanous ivory nightgown her mother would have chosen for her wedding trousseau. Aja had a voluptuous figure then. As she stood before me in the candlelight of the bedroom that night, I imagined her in a silky black Victoria's Secret gown hugging her ample curves.

"Aja, you're so beautiful."

I wanted her. I had hoped she wanted me, too. She came to me and let me kiss her. Our lips barely touched. I felt the delight of passion rising inside me. This would be an arousing slow dance as I courted my new bride.

I kissed her again, teasing her mouth open with the tip of my tongue. I slipped a finger under the wide strap of her gown and stroked her shoulder. I kissed her neck. Gentle kisses.

I pressed against her.

She flinched and pulled away.

"Aja, we'll go slow," I assured her. "Come, my darling."

"No, Kamal."

"No? No to what?"

"Everything. Not tonight."

I was speechless. A groom rebuffed on his wedding night.

We were ensconced in a three-room suite at the luxurious Taj Mahal Palace Hotel. The post-wedding gala continued in a grand ballroom on another floor. Were our mothers sitting together with the other women at the party, fanning themselves as they envisioned what might be transpiring in the bridal suite? A laughable thought, as I sat on the divan in the suite's sitting room that night, finishing off the Taj's best champagne. When I awoke the next morning from my bed on the divan, the bottle was afloat in the bucket.

I looked to the bedroom. The door was still closed.

Our marriage slowly recovered from its horrible start. Aja barely tolerated sex. When she got pregnant with Yamir eight months after the wedding, there was much rejoicing in our families. But I knew our sex life was over for nine months and far longer – maybe forever, unless or until she wanted another child.

When I met Liz at Charles de Gaulle Airport, I hadn't been a faithful husband. I had strayed regularly during my travels, looking for any opportunity to take a woman to bed. The worst part, I didn't feel ashamed. I had a burning need for sex and wasn't getting it from my wife. A man needs a woman. I was responding to my biology. I had no regrets or remorse.

I had just unhooked the wheels of our luggage carts when I asked Liz if she was staying in Paris. Even if she were on a layover, it would be easy to take her to my hotel room. I liked transiting through Charles de Gaulle. I always booked a room at the Sheraton. The staff knew me. Perhaps it was no accident that the bellman had taken Liz's luggage to my room. I suppose he had assumed she and I would end up there. I hadn't pre-arranged that, but I certainly didn't mind. I knew I had a bit of a reputation there. The room-service delivery staff had tales to tell about my bedmates. One playful young lady had hung her red bra on the room's door handle, to guide the cart-pusher to us at three in the morning. She didn't want him knocking on the wrong door by mistake at such an ungodly hour.

I had become an ungodly man in the eyes of my father, who had guessed at my secret life. I think he, too, had strayed from time to time in his life with my mother. But his anger with me stemmed from the dishonor I brought the family when I came home one Christmas and announced my engagement to the British rose. Lily was her name.

My father threatened to disown me. I walked out on him, defying and defiling him and his old ways, and returned to Lily's bed in London. A few months later, he sent a telegram — a *telegram* — informing me my mother had suffered a breakdown. She had been taken to a psychiatric hospital. *If you love her, you'll have the decency to come to her bedside. STOP.*

There was no stopping the emotional tsunami that reached my distant shore and swept me home. The only peace to be made was to marry Aja. I hated my family and hers. I pitied her that she couldn't say no to their machinations. She knew of my engagement to Lily. But she let herself be the pawn in the drama that erupted: Her family contending I had disgraced her. Mine damning me for that, but claiming I would do the honorable thing and marry her.

And so it was that I landed on the divan on my wedding night.

After I said good-bye to Liz, I stood in the lobby at the Sheraton's elevator bank, for an eternity it seemed. Finally, the doors opened and I joined the herd pressing for space in the car, wishing she were with me.

When I got back to my room, I saw something on the floor by the bed where Liz's bags had been. It was a small journal. I suddenly was struck by a whim.

Why the hell not?

I sprinted down the corridor and slammed the elevator's down arrow. Precious seconds ticked away.

Ten minutes later, I was on the train – hopefully, *her* train – moments before they closed the doors. The cars were packed with students and tourists. Luggage was mounded at the end of the car, making it impossible for me to pass. I could have scaled the baggage mound. I was a smitten man, yes – but not desperate. I was on Liz's train to Provence, I hoped. In a little more than two hours, my journey would end in joy or folly.

LIZ

I WAS DEEP in the fog of jet lag when the train pulled into Avignon station. I grabbed my bags from the pile at the end of the car. There hadn't been an empty seat in the first-class coach. It was high season and the train seemed to bulge with its passengers and cargo. I'm not sure how that hulk of metal managed to attain the high speeds it's famous for. But I just managed to catch a glimpse of sunflower fields in their full bloom as we sped through the countryside at 250 km/hour.

I had never been to Avignon, so I had to summon every functioning cell of my brain as I stepped onto the platform. I looked for *sortie* signs, but decided to follow the masses.

I stopped short at the stairs leading to the station terminal below, wondering if I should opt for the elevator.

It was then that I saw him.

I thought for sure my foggy brain was playing tricks on me. But there he stood on the platform, with his hands in the pockets of his jeans, smiling at me.

Kamal slowly walked toward me. "Surprised?" he asked.

I nodded. "Very."

"It was an impulse. A reckless one."

I felt suspended between worlds – the real one and the one invented by my lustful imagination.

"I can get the next train back to Paris." He looked longingly at me.

"Why?"

He grinned. "I was hoping you'd say that." He reached for the handle of my suitcase. "May I take this? As you can see, I travel light."

"You brought nothing?"

"Nothing. I barely had time to make the train."

Our first challenge came within minutes. We knew virtually nothing about each other as we faced the interrogator at the Europcar counter. When the agent asked if I wanted to add Kamal as a driver, I turned to him. Kamal nodded and quickly presented his passport and driver's license. The agent asked for his date of birth.

"May 28," he said.

"Really? That's my mother's birthday."

Kamal smiled.

As we walked to the car, he said to me, laughing, "You need to pretend like you know me."

We still had an hour's drive before we reached my destination, high on the Luberon plateau. We stopped for lunch in Goult, a lovely, sleepy village perched on a rocky hilltop that overlooks a vista of fruit orchards and vineyards. Tour buses don't come to Goult, which makes it feel like a hidden gem. I discovered Goult on my first visit to the Luberon and enjoyed wandering its quiet, narrow streets bordered by stone houses with doors and shutters painted from the palette of the countryside – pale olive green, cornflower blue and vibrant lavender.

The main hub of the village is a bistro-bar called Café de la Poste. Lunch there is a social event. Most tables are reserved for regulars or large family groups. Few tourists are in the mix. The clientele is well-heeled – French and English mostly. The women tend to wear noticeable jewelry and carry expensive designer handbags.

We wangled a small table under the shade of the umbrellas. I ordered gazpacho and a hearty salad with warmed goat cheese on toasted bread – *salade chèvre chaud*. Kamal had *croque monsieur*. We were fortifying ourselves for what was to come. I was already aching for what was to come.

Suddenly, the genteel ambiance was shattered when a middle-aged woman jumped up from her seat and started ranting in French. I couldn't make out what she was saying, but many in the crowd were amused. I tried to imagine what had set her off. Her anger was directed at a man and woman, seated at a table next to us. Maybe the guy was her husband, with his mistress. Or maybe he was her lover who had taken his wife out to lunch. Or maybe he was her ex-husband with his new girlfriend. In France, the possibilities are many.

Two waiters whisked her away, shushing her.

"Love the local entertainment," Kamal said.

He reached across the table and took my hand. "Are you okay with this? Me, showing up here."

I hesitated. I was more than okay. But I felt a bit jittery. I hadn't been with a man since my divorce.

"I have something for you." He pulled my travel journal from a pocket of his jacket.

"Where did you get that?" I asked.

"I found it on the floor of my room. It must have fallen out of your suitcase pocket when the bellman brought up your bags."

"Hope he didn't read it." I smiled at Kamal.

"I did. On the train."

My eyes widened. Kamal laughed.

"I came to Avignon to deliver this," he said, handing me the journal. "I can hitch a ride back to the station."

"You're going to make me say how much I want you to stay, aren't you?"

He smiled. "I would like to hear that." He squeezed my hand. "Come. Let's take a walk. Show me Goult."

We walked through the village, to the top of the hill.

"Close your eyes," I told Kamal, as we rounded the last bend. I held a hand at his back as I guided him up the last stretch of the street.

"I like this." He put an arm around my shoulder as we walked together.

At the top, I said, "Now open your eyes."

We were standing in front of the village's ancient windmill, which isn't visible from the main approach to Goult. The panoramic view of the valley below is incredible from this spot.

"Wow." Kamal took it all in for a few moments, then turned to me, holding my face in his hands. "*This* is a big wow."

He kissed me. We quickly decided, after a few more kisses, it was urgently necessary to get to the B&B as soon as possible.

KAMAL

I FELL FAST for Liz.

She couldn't have been more adorable when we arrived at the B&B. She was new to this place, although she had visited the Luberon a couple of times before. It was good the owner didn't know her, which helped her concoct our story — the boyfriend who had surprised her and would be staying with her for a few days. I desperately wanted to stay the entire week she had booked. But I was already facing a concocted explanation to my wife.

The owner showed us to our room, the Red Room. How apropos, I thought.

He didn't linger, thankfully. I closed the windows and turned on the fan. It was a warm day, so unlike the dreary weather we had left in Paris.

Liz stood in the middle of the room. Her gorgeous auburn hair had a fiery glow in the late afternoon light. For a moment, she reminded me of timid Aja on our wedding night. But I knew Liz wanted me.

I caressed her as I undressed her. She undid my shirt, fumbling nervously with the buttons. Then she unbuckled my belt. I made quick work of shedding my jeans and briefs.

I laid her on the bed and pulled off her panties. She was warm and wet.

I knew I was swimming in deep, churning waters with Liz. But I had never felt so alive.

LIZ

My first visit to the Luberon had been the summer after my divorce, in 2013. It was July and to my delight, the lavender was in full bloom. A happy accident.

My divorce had been soul sucking. I wasn't sure I would ever heal. But that summer, wandering in the lavender fields helped restore me.

I had a big tub at the B&B where I stayed on that first visit. Every morning, I'd soak there, crumbling fresh lavender into the warm bath water. At night, when all the other guests had gone to bed, I'd slip out to the pool just outside my room and swim naked. I desperately needed to cleanse the blackness from my heart.

My work often brought me to Europe. The next year, I timed my summer travel around the lavender bloom. The Luberon had become my corner of paradise.

I loved exploring the Luberon's high plateaus where the lavender fields sprawl to the horizon line. I nearly cried the first time I saw a harvesting machine reduce a postcard-perfect field to green stubble. But as the air suddenly turned to perfume, I felt intoxicated.

When Kamal and I awoke the first morning in the Red Room, I felt another kind of intoxication. I was in the clutches of primal hormones. My desire for Kamal felt more animal than human. I couldn't get enough of him. And he gladly gave me what I wanted.

That first morning, we barely managed to get showered – I had never known the soapy bliss of an orgasm at the hands of a man who already knew every square inch of me. We reluctantly got dressed, tempted to fall back into bed. But we were both starving.

Breakfast was a comedy. Luc, the proprietor, asked how we liked our eggs. I looked at Kamal. I had no idea how he liked his eggs. He ordered poached. I like mine scrambled. I offered him the pitcher of warm milk for his coffee. He shook his head and smiled. "By tomorrow, you'll know everything about me."

Black coffee and poached eggs. And toast dripping with butter and honey. I had so much more to learn about this man, whose cart had locked wheels with mine. I wanted to know *everything* about him.

We set out that morning for the village of Sault, about 20 miles north of the B&B. The route to Sault cuts through a gorge, along a cliff-hugging road of hairpin turns. When we stopped at an overlook, Kamal offered to drive, to my relief.

Sault is situated on a hillside overlooking a patchwork of lavender fields dotted with brightly colored apiaries and stuccoed farmhouses in shades of apricot and sandstone. I had read in a guidebook, before my first visit, that the valley below Sault "presents one of the loveliest landscapes in France." That was no overstatement.

I'm probably not the first visitor to the Luberon who drove off the road at the first glimpse of a lavender field. I jumped out of my rental car, two wheels in the ditch, and what happened next was nothing short of a spiritual experience. I carefully stepped between the mounded rows, my feet sinking into the rocky soil. A goat's bell chimed in the distance, accompanying a choir of humming bees and those boisterous, singing *cigales*, the French cousins of cicadas I remember from childhood summers in rural Virginia.

Kamal stopped the car at the edge of a field, with a view of Sault in the distance. He took my hand as we walked into the field together. I picked a lavender sprig and gently squeezed the plump flower bud. I held it to his nose.

"Ahhh. Heaven," he said. "I've learned something important about you." He pulled me close.

"What's that?" I slipped the lavender blossom in his shirt pocket.

"You live life with all your senses." He kissed me. "I love the taste of you. I think there's a little lavender honey left over from breakfast." He touched the corner of my mouth. "Were you saving this for me?"

"Mm-hmm."

Lavender honey. One of the decadent delights of the Luberon.

Bees hummed close by as they sipped nectar from the sticky purple blooms.

The piercing call of the *cigales* was almost unnerving. The *cigale* is the emblem of the Luberon. It looks like a huge cricket, with bulging eyes and beautiful lacy wings. The song of the *cigales* heralds the arrival of hot summer days. The vociferous males vibrate abdominal membranes called "tymbals" to seduce their mates. These guys are LOUD. Their girlfriends probably have significant hearing loss.

The mating vibration wasn't lost on Kamal and me, as he led me back to the car. He drove down a deserted dirt road and parked under a stand of shade trees.

"What are you up to?" I asked him teasingly.

He leaned over and kissed me. "I'll meet you in the back seat."

Our little Clio rocked with the rhythmic motion of us. The night before, during one of our short-lived respites in the Red Room, Kamal had asked me about my sexual fantasies. One of my favorites is lying naked in a forest on a carpet of moss, looking up at the treetops, as the blinding wave of my climax comes. On my forest bed, I have no inhibitions. I easily give myself to wanton erotic pleasure and let my unthrottled moans echo through the forest.

I lived my fantasy, without the carpet of moss, that afternoon in the Clio. The only thing louder was the *cigales*.

KAMAL

My few days with Liz in Provence were amazing. Incredible sex. Laughs. Breathtaking beauty – the scenery wasn't bad either. Great food. And incredible sex. Right, I already said that.

I was in big trouble. I had called Aja twice, telling her both times I had to stay in Paris another day. The meetings weren't going well – I needed more time to close the deal, I told her. Total bullshit.

Truth is, I didn't have a meeting planned during my stopover in Paris. I was just looking for another bedmate at the Sheraton for a night.

I hated myself for this secret life of mine. But it was the only way I had been able to keep my sanity in a loveless, sexless marriage.

I missed Yamir. He had a little cold and was cranky when I called the second night. "Daddy, when are you coming home?"

I had been away almost three weeks. I knew I had to get back to London. But I couldn't bear telling Liz I had to go.

She was stoic about it and kindly offered to drive me to Avignon.

I promised her I'd come see her in Paris and would help her get settled, if she needed me. "This is not good-bye."

My lasting image of Liz during our three days together in the Luberon was of her dancing in a field of lavender. One morning at breakfast, Luc had mapped out for us a single-track road through a lavender production area near Lagarde-d'Apt. As I turned down the rutted road, a vast purple field stretched before us. In the distance, rising majestically above streaks of clouds, we could see...

"The Alps!" Liz exclaimed. "Kamal, stop the car! Those are the Alps!"

She sprang out of the Clio and ran into the field, with the Alps behind her, twirling and singing like Julie Andrews in the opening scene of *The Sound of Music*.

I smiled as I watched her, loving her joyful abandon and the way she embraced life through every pore of her being.

She had become, in short order, part of my heart and soul. I knew I was screwed. But in a very good way.

LIZ

When I left Kamal at the station in Avignon, I stood on the platform watching his train disappear into nothingness, not quite sure I hadn't dreamt the whole thing.

I felt both exhilarated and unsettled.

He wasn't quite out of earshot when he called his wife the first day to tell her he needed to stay longer in Paris. I could tell by the way he spoke to her that lying came naturally to him. He didn't hesitate or stumble as he invented his story. He did this a lot, it seemed. I suspected his business meeting at the Sheraton might have been a lie, too.

But I didn't care.

Our bedroom for three days was filled with our stories and laughter. Our bed was strewn with lavender petals and pastry flakes. One afternoon as Kamal unhooked my bra, crusty caramelized crumbs from a *sacristan* fell to the floor.

"You are my delicious puff pastry," he murmured, licking the baker's sugary bits from my skin.

I knew we would see each other again. He called every day during the rest of my stay in Provence. He wanted to know if I missed him.

I more than missed him. One night, he called very late. We had phone sex. He told me he was in the study of his London townhouse. Aja was asleep in their bed two floors above.

"I must be quiet," he whispered into the phone. "But not you." I closed the windows of the Red Room and laid myself on the bed. I took off my wispy nightgown and sprawled naked on the bedsheets, letting the baritone timbre of Kamal's voice arouse me.

I understood why boys' voices drop as they enter puberty, when everything that happens to them at that age is about the laws of attraction. Words of seduction and love are articulated through thickened vocal chords that, at a lower vibration, assure the continuation of the human race. A brilliant piece of evolution. Like the male *cigales* rubbing their abdominal membranes to vociferously attract a mate, Kamal tuned his vibration to the molten core of me.

As I lay on the damp sheets after we said good night in the wee hours, I thought of the Pierre Bonnard painting I had come to France to investigate. The subjects of his pictures ranged from bowls of vibrantly colored fruit to erotic nudes.

His frequent model was his lover, Marthe de Méligny, who after a 32-year relationship with Bonnard became his wife in 1925. At the time of their marriage she was 56; he was 58.

Marthe often posed naked for him, without inhibition – sponging her inner thighs above a washbasin or wearing only heels, standing with her back to him, in front of a glowing fireplace. She shed her clothes – and he did the same – in photographs they took of each other in their garden. Bonnard often obscured Marthe's face in his paintings of her, focusing on her petite, well-toned body, her muscular buttocks and small upturned breasts. He infused her alabaster skin with a palette of pastels.

His sensual depictions of Marthe in their bed aren't classical nudes in the style of Manet's *Olympia* or Ingres' *La Grande Odalisque*. Bonnard gives a voyeur's view of his lover, with legs splayed apart in his painting of her called *Indolence*. His own imprint is still on the tangled sheets. She smiles coyly at him, with one arm behind her head, the other resting beneath her breasts.

Their relationship was tortured in the years before their marriage. Another woman came on the scene. Her name was Renée Monchaty, a young artist whom Bonnard met in 1916. He used Renée as a model and eventually they became lovers. She sometimes spent time with Bonnard and Marthe at their home in the French hamlet of Vernonnet, in Normandy, across the Seine from the town of Vernon. In the early 1920s, Bonnard began a painting of the two women together, called *Young Women in the Garden,* in which he pitted them against each other on canvas as the rivals they were in his life. In September 1925, a few weeks after Bonnard married Marthe, forsaken Renée committed suicide.

Shattered by his affair, Marthe insisted that Bonnard destroy his paintings of Renée. But instead, he hid them away. After Marthe's death in 1942, some art historians believe he re-visited those paintings, including *Young Women in the Garden*, turning Renée's brown hair blond. Perhaps to help obscure her memory – or gild it.

The painting that went off at auction at Sotheby's created a stir in the art world. It had been privately owned by the Chastain family who had lived for a century in the village of Giverny, where Bonnard's friend Claude Monet resided for the last half of his life, only a few kilometers from Vernonnet. Bonnard supposedly had given the painting to his gardener, André Chastain, after Renée's suicide. It is indisputably the most sexual of Bonnard's boudoir nudes. The voluptuous Renée lies naked in a rumpled bed, her full breasts and flushed face illuminated by candlelight. She rests a hand at her crotch, as if prolonging her pleasure for the man painting her. A shocking scene in its day, no doubt.

But what's even more shocking is an almost indiscernible image that appears in the shadowy corner of the room. Nearly obscured by the brocade curtains is Marthe, witness to her lover's and her rival's beastly betrayal.

Vernonnet, France ~ Spring 2014

SYLVIE

HE RANG THE bell promptly at eleven. I'll never forget my first glimpse of Émile, as I opened the gate. The breeze of a March day had slightly tousled his graying chestnut hair. But everything else about him was impeccable. He had the suave sophistication of a Parisian, but there was nothing foppish or vain about him. He had a warm smile and firm handshake. I liked him instantly.

It was not my job to give tours of the house. But Madame and Monsieur Lambert were out of town for a few days and had asked me to show him around. He was a Paris art dealer with good references. I didn't mind playing hostess. In fact, it was a nice diversion from my routine as the housekeeper of a charming little house on the Seine where Pierre Bonnard had once lived.

I didn't tell Émile that morning that my grandfather had been the gardener during Bonnard's years here. I didn't think he'd be interested in that.

He told me he had come to nearby Giverny for a meeting with the Impressionist museum there, about an exhibition they were mounting. He worked with museums in helping them locate paintings in private collections. His clients were some of the world's most affluent, astute collectors of Impressionist and Post-Impressionist art, he told me that day.

I showed him around the house and property. He was intrigued by the careful attention to detail the Lamberts had paid to decorating the house according to Bonnard's photographs and paintings of the home's interiors.

Émile asked about the tub in the bathroom downstairs, a close replica of the one Marthe posed in for many of Bonnard's paintings.

"Is this the original?" he asked incredulously.

"No. But a good copy, *oui*?" I didn't tell him that the original tub had been relocated to what's now my bathroom, in my family's residence in Giverny. When Bonnard sold the house and moved to southern France in 1939, he gave the tub to my grandfather, André.

After my improvised tour, Émile invited me to join him for lunch at Giverny's historic Hôtel Baudy, where American Impressionist painters resided during Monet's time. The Baudy no longer offers accommodations, but it's a bustling place at meal times during the tourist season. Little goes unnoticed by the locals who gather at the Baudy. My entrance with Émile that day certainly got attention.

It was a lovely lunch. Émile spared no expense, ordering pricey wine and three courses. The wine went to my head, I must admit, along with his compliments. It was nice to be the recipient of so much appreciative male attention.

In my 20s, I had been married to a shiftless Parisian man. He was a good lover and was adored in the trendy clubs of Paris that we frequented. I thought then that we had it all. But in time, I saw we had nothing. Nothing in common. Nothing that could support a life together. He started hitting on barmaids, even when I was looking. I came back to Giverny, humiliated. My parents took me in. I knew my father wanted to tell me how foolish I had been not to listen to his warnings about my choice of a husband.

After my divorce, I worked in Vernon, at the museum there and later at the tourist bureau. I took the job at the Bonnard house when Madame and Monsieur Lambert bought the property a few years ago. The Lamberts, both in their 70s, had owned a Paris gallery for many years and enjoyed entertaining their many friends in the art world. I often helped out at their parties, which gave me a social life I didn't have otherwise.

But that day at the Baudy, I hoped that might change. I let myself succumb to Émile's charm that afternoon. And why not? I knew he was a lot younger – only 50, I learned later. But what does age matter after 50? I was still attractive at 59. I'd kept myself in shape. I looked good in my stylish clothes, which I chose carefully, within my budget constraints, on occasional shopping trips to Paris. Well traveled and educated, I was nobody's fool. Or so I had always thought.

I'd had a number of romances over the years. Some lasted a year or two with the promise of something permanent. But nothing lasted. The endings were often bitter disappointments for me. I'd swear off men for a while. But then a man would come along who made me believe that true love had finally found me.

Émile made me feel I was the most captivating woman in the room. He was full of questions and interested to hear that my family had lived in Giverny for more than a century.

"*Vraiment?*" His eyes lit up. "They were here during Monet's time?"

I nodded. And then I told him my grandfather had worked for Bonnard.

He seemed surprised. "To think that I'm here with you, twice removed from Bonnard himself."

I laughed. "That was a *long* time ago. Before the Second World War."

He impulsively reached for my hand. "Not *that* long ago, Sylvie. Think of it."

He held my hand gently in his. That was the moment when all the trouble began.

ÉMILE

I KNEW ABOUT Sylvie's grandfather, the groundskeeper, before I met her. That's why I went to the Bonnard house that day, hoping I'd get to talk with her and find out more. I was grateful that the owners were away so that I could give Sylvie my full attention.

I hadn't expected she would be so enchanting.

After lunch that afternoon, I asked her to join me for a stroll through the Baudy's back garden, where American Impressionist painters back in the day used to set up their easels. The winding pathways lead up through terraced plantings that offer secluded places to sit and enjoy the view.

We had just polished off a bottle of Bordeaux between us at lunch. The March air was a bit chilly. It felt natural for me to offer her my arm and keep her close to me, as we walked up the stone steps.

I think she would have let me kiss her in the garden that day. She was feeling the effects of the wine, I could tell by her rosy cheeks.

But I didn't want to rush things.

I asked if I could call her. Maybe we could meet in Paris soon? I'd take her to Ladurée on the Champs Élysées for lunch.

Of course, she said yes.

⌒

We met a week later at Ladurée. She looked stunning in a vermilion-red suit that offset her sleek dark hair, streaked with silvery strands, and was wearing a shade of lipstick that matched her ensemble. She was slimmer than she appeared when I met her. She had been wearing loose-fitting trousers and a tunic sweater that day. Her waist and legs were thin. She flashed a confident smile as I kissed her on each cheek. I caught a whiff of L'Air du Temps. A chic woman scented with vintage perfume. I liked that combination.

We started lunch with champagne and ended with tea and Ladurée's famous *macarons*. She clearly enjoyed my company. We made another date for the following week when I'd be back in Giverny for the installation of the exhibit.

I hoped this was the beginning of a delightful little affair.

July 2015

LIZ

I WAS GLAD to have had my Luberon respite before tackling the work at hand back in Paris. But even in my shady spot by the pool, I had already set up a makeshift office with my Bonnard books on the wicker table by the chaise. I read about his life, his work, his affairs, as I made notes riddled with question marks and asterisks.

Bonnard grew up outside of Paris in an upper middle-class family. His father, a civil servant at the War Ministry, pressured him to become a lawyer. While in law school, Bonnard took painting courses at Académie Julian, where he and several of his classmates, including Édouard Vuillard, Maurice Denis and Paul Sérusier, formed a group called Les Nabis – Hebrew for "prophets." Inspired by the work of Post-Impressionist painter Paul Gauguin, the Nabis artists embraced decorative and abstract motifs found in poster designs, book illustrations, tapestries, frescoes and Japanese art. In 1889, Bonnard won a design competition for a French Champagne poster that soon was seen on advertisement kiosks all over Paris. The Nabis group organized its first exhibition in 1891, and Bonnard received praise as a skillful decorative artist.

Bonnard became a licensed attorney, but abandoned a legal career to focus on art. He was working as a book illustrator and a lithographer in 1893, when he met Marthe on a Paris street, the story goes, soon after she had arrived in Paris. She had left behind her family and low-class past in her hometown of Saint-Amand-Montrond, in rural central France. She told Bonnard she was 16 — when, in fact, she was 24, just two years younger than he. Whether Bonnard sensed her lie or didn't care about bedding a teenager, he became her lover and she became his frequent model. He didn't learn of her real name — Maria Boursin — until they married in 1925. She had adopted the more aristocratic-sounding name Marthe de Méligny to conceal her humble roots, as she re-invented herself in her new Parisian life.

He and Marthe eventually left Paris, preferring seclusion in the nearby countryside. I was intrigued with Bonnard's reclusiveness, which seemed, in part, a concession to Marthe, whose mental and physical frailties are frequently noted by art historians. She bathed compulsively — several times a day — giving Bonnard ample opportunity to observe her lying in the tub, washing herself, drying her body and spritzing it with perfume. Some historians speculate she had a skin problem or perhaps a cleanliness obsession. Bonnard never painted the details of her face. When they were out walking together in Paris, she would shield herself with an umbrella so that she wouldn't be seen. She's often described in her later years as neurotic and paranoid. But Bonnard clearly was enamored, at least with his early memories of her. Even as she aged, her body never lost its youthfulness in his flattering depictions of her.

One afternoon at the B&B, I had the pool to myself. The *cigales* were rasping as I floated on my back, the sun warming my face. I pretended I was Marthe, soaking in her shallow tub. Her alabaster skin was the color of the clear water, unlike mine, which was getting darker by the day. One art historian likened her bathtub poses to a corpse in a marble sarcophagus. Maybe she was just having a nice long soak, I thought. My lavender baths each evening were hardly funereal. Quite the opposite. I wasn't dead to the world. I was soaking up the perfume of *mon petit paradis*. I had learned to read art-historian interpretations with grains of bath salts, realizing how the subjective reaction to art takes on the beholder's bias, however twisted or tainted.

As I floated in the pool, I imagined Bonnard's first encounter with Marthe on a Paris street, him seizing a moment of opportunity. Not unlike Kamal.

Did Kamal intentionally lock his cart's wheels with mine? Perhaps I'll never know. But he made the most of that moment of opportunity that led us on a life-altering course.

I was sorry to say good-bye to my Red Room. I promised Luc I would be back the next summer.

When I arrived at my Paris apartment, the painters were still whitewashing the walls. But they said I could camp in a corner for a couple of days while they finished. I didn't need to be there much during the day. I quickly unpacked what little I had brought and soon felt at home.

I loved the space. It was one huge room with a high ceiling and slanted windows at the roofline that flooded the apartment with diffused light, filtered through swags of loosely woven cloth. It had been used for years as a painter's studio and recently had been acquired by the Musée d'Orsay as an apartment for visiting researchers.

The furnishings were standard IKEA issue. It suited my needs just fine. The bed had a good mattress. The kitchen installation was more than adequate. Lots of cupboards, counter space and a big fridge.

What I loved most were the expansive walls, perfect for hanging posters of Bonnard's work. I always surround myself with an artist's paintings when I work on a forgery case. They become trusted friends. Only color-accurate prints will do. I want every detail to be true to the originals so that I can more easily spot a clue of an impostor. After the fresh paint dried, I would poster-paper the walls of what would be my new home for a while.

I had no idea how long I'd be in Paris. Sotheby's had made the arrangements with the Orsay for my office space there and the apartment, which was on a quiet side street in Saint-Germain-des-Prés. I guessed that I had at least a month of research ahead of me. The judge reviewing the forgery case had granted a delay in the proceedings for me to do my work. But the clock was ticking.

On the first night after the painting crew had finished, I set up a projector with a carousel tray full of slides I had borrowed from the museum archives. I prefer high-quality museum slides to digital images, for their razor-sharp resolution and natural color.

I poured myself a glass of wine and turned off the lights. I sat back on my comfy IKEA sofa and let the slide show begin, immersing myself in the sensuous world of Pierre Bonnard.

April 2014

SYLVIE

My grandfather once told me it was difficult to watch those two tortured women. There was something animal about their behavior, he said. The way they eyed each other, the way they seemed to sniff at each other, claws bared beneath their raised fur.

Madame Lambert had hung a framed print of Bonnard's painting *Young Women in the Garden* above her desk in the sitting room. I found it unsettling to see the young Renée – with her postmortem halo of blond curls – smiling at Bonnard, while Marthe, in darkened profile, is a barely noticeable onlooker in the lower right corner of the picture.

In one of the art books Madame Lambert kept on the table of the sitting room, there was a large color photo of Bonnard's *The Terrace at Vernonnet*, his last painting of the house before he and Marthe moved to southern France in 1939. The setting is the terrace just inside the front gate, at the top of the stairs leading to the garden below. The scene seems idyllic at first glance. It appears there's a party in progress. The hostess, dressed in apricot, is most likely Marthe. She stands at a linen-covered table, where a bottle of wine and a platter of fruit have been placed. A shorter woman, in blue, stands behind her, holding a basket of plums. To the left of a massive tree trunk that divides the foreground of the painting, a few guests stand on the balcony of the house. But when the eye roams to the far right of the canvas, the garden party seems about to take a violent turn. A woman at the edge of the canvas looks to be chiseled from stone, in a warrior pose. Standing behind a bench, she has her arm raised, holding the handle of what appears to be a hatchet – some say it's a tennis racket. If true, she's about to make a punishing serve. The consensus is that this seemingly vengeful woman is Renée, who at the time of this painting had been dead for 14 years.

I heard my grandfather say that Bonnard had never forgiven himself for Renée's death. He was old enough to be her father, but he seduced her and fell passionately in love. Renée was his enchantress, the object of his obsessive desire. He proposed to Renée and took her to Rome, where he met her parents and asked their permission to marry her. But Marthe had her hooks in him and, in the end, he couldn't bear to leave her. Renée was devastated when he broke the news to her that he would marry Marthe instead. The legendary tale of Renée's suicide is that she died in her bathtub. But my grandfather said that she covered her bed with flower petals and lay there for her last breaths before she shot herself in the head.

It was almost impossible to imagine a sordid love triangle casting such a pall over this tranquil place. I stepped from the sitting room — which had been Bonnard's studio in his day — onto the balcony with its distinctive crosshatched white railing and smelled the first whiffs of spring. The fruit trees were blooming. I was giddy with happiness. I had a dinner date that night with Émile.

I hadn't felt this way in years. Émile would be coming at six. We would have a cocktail at the Baudy bar or maybe out on the terrace under the linden trees. He said he wanted to keep our dinner location a surprise.

I fussed with the knot of my scarf. I jumped when I heard the bell ring at the gate. He was 10 minutes early. A good sign, I thought. He was eager, too.

ÉMILE

I TOOK SYLVIE to Le Jardin des Plumes for dinner that night. It's the priciest restaurant in Giverny. I spared no expense. I was seducing her. I'm not ashamed to say that. I found her attractive.

In the candle glow at our secluded corner table, I imagined her naked. Her silk scarf drew my attention to the low neckline of her form-fitting black dress. She filled out that dress nicely. I wanted to unzip her and let that little black dress fall to the floor.

I could tell she wanted me. I reached across the table at one point during dinner and stroked the top of her hand. She turned it upward toward mine, inviting my touch.

It was late, about eleven, when we left the restaurant. I pulled up at her house, situated behind a stone wall, on a sloping lane below the main street of the village. She invited me inside for a nightcap and suggested I park in the back, by the garage.

We walked through the rear garden and entered the house through the back door. She flipped on a switch, which lit a lamp over the kitchen table. A bowl of lemons and oranges sat on a blue-checked cloth. Blue delft tiles lined the backsplash of the sink. Copper pots hung from a rack over the stove. It reminded me of the kitchen at Monet's house.

I helped her take off her coat. And of course, that was it. I pulled her toward me for the kiss she clearly wanted.

She poured cognac. And we headed upstairs to her bedroom.

July 2015

KAMAL

It didn't take long for Aja to suspect another woman.

A couple of days after I returned home from my tryst with Liz in the Luberon, I found my underwear folded in a neat pile on my side of the bed. I thought that was odd. Usually, Aja put my underwear and socks in the dresser.

On top of the underwear was a sprig of lavender that apparently had gone through the wash.

I wasn't aware that Aja was standing in the bedroom doorway, behind me, as I sniffed the washed-out petals. She startled me when she spoke. "I found that in a pocket when I was ironing one of your shirts."

I vaguely remembered Liz holding a lavender bud for me to smell. Maybe she had tucked it into my pocket as I kissed her.

"I was walking through Place des Vosges," I said nonchalantly. "There are lavender plantings there. The scent was incredible."

Aja turned away, without speaking. Yamir was calling for her.

A few nights later, I heard her coming down the stairs at 2 a.m. when I was on a call with Liz. Phone sex had quickly become our habit.

I clicked off the call and pretended to be asleep on the sofa where I was lying. I quickly zipped myself up as the door opened slowly. Aja didn't turn on the light. But she stood in the dark for a minute and then quietly left, closing the door behind her.

The next morning at breakfast, she asked, "Kamal, why are you in the study late at night?"

"I'm having trouble sleeping. I don't want to disturb you."

"Why can't you sleep?" she asked.

"Work."

"Is there a problem?"

"That Paris deal is going sideways."

"What will you do?"

"I may need to go back for a few days."

Aja meticulously spread peanut butter on a slice of toast for Yamir. When she looked up at me, I knew she knew.

A week later, as I got off the Eurostar train at the Gare du Nord station, I was surprised to see a platoon of soldiers, armed with machine guns, on the platform. Ever since the Charlie Hebdo attack back in January, police were everywhere around Paris. But this was the first time I had seen soldiers in combat gear.

I grabbed a cab and got to Liz's apartment just as she was coming up the sidewalk.

"You're here!" She ran into my arms.

I held her tight. "God, I've missed you."

She took me upstairs. There was no chatter over a drink, as a prelude. We just went crazy. Our sexual appetites had become insatiable. There's a huge danger in that, when all caution is lost.

But I didn't care about the danger. All I wanted was Liz. All of her.

LIZ

Kamal was sprawled naked on my bed, still half asleep, as I bent down to kiss him good-bye that morning.

He squinted, trying to focus. "You're leaving me already?"

I laughed. "Only for a few hours."

"Where are you going?"

"I have a date with Pierre Bonnard."

"Should I be jealous?" He gently pulled me onto the bed.

"He's not my type."

Kamal kissed me. "Am I?"

"You have great potential."

It was my first meeting with the Orsay's Impressionist Art curator. I knew she would be questioning the results of the tests ordered by the Chinese buyer. She had been one of the curators present on the day Sotheby's viewed the painting at the Chastain residence in Giverny. She, herself, had thought it was an original.

She informed me that Sotheby's had authenticated Bonnard's signature before the auction. "They say it's a perfect match to other works he did at that time."

I wouldn't be satisfied with that finding until I had done my own assessment. But I said nothing.

"When will we get the analysis of the paint samples?" I asked.

"In a couple of weeks. They're running a few extra tests."

She gave me a tour of a storeroom where several of the museum's Bonnards were in napping mode. Paintings often are stored for a time, allowing them to rest in a climate-controlled environment. Periodically, they're examined by conservators to check for deterioration.

The Orsay had just held a Bonnard exhibition, so there were many more of his paintings in the storeroom that day waiting to be shipped back to donor museums, which gave me an excellent opportunity to see a vast collection of his work.

Bonnard clearly separated himself from the avant-garde art movements of the early 1900s. In his reclusive life away from Paris with Marthe, Bonnard developed what became known as his "Intimist" style, focusing on domestic scenes, as well as still lifes and garden landscapes. He infused his paintings with exquisite color that expressed a wide range of moods and emotions. He abandoned linear perspective – a teacup seems to sit precariously on a table, as if it might slide off the canvas. It's a device that essentially brings the viewer into the picture and Bonnard's private world.

The Sotheby's painting, which had been given the title *Renée*, certainly was in keeping with his intimate bedroom nudes of Marthe, whom he had depicted in dreamy post-coital bliss in her youth. But unlike the early Marthe nudes, *Renée* crackled with sexuality.

Renée was in her late teens when she began modeling for Bonnard. According to some accounts, she had been in a relationship with American painter Harry Lachman, who, years later, became a Hollywood film director. Her youthful beauty undoubtedly invigorated Bonnard, who, then in his 50s, longed to escape his claustrophobic, melancholic existence with Marthe.

Renée's visits to Vernonnet added a sadistic twist to the story. It was easy to imagine how she might have flaunted her sex appeal, as middle-aged Marthe stood by, watching helplessly from the margins of the canvas. The *ménage à trois* threw Marthe into jealous rages. She threatened to kill herself when she learned of Bonnard's plans to marry Renée. But it was the young seductress who took her life. In one chilling account I read, Bonnard himself found Renée dead in her bathtub. I wondered if she had drugged herself and drowned, or had she slit her wrists and bled to death? Regardless, there had been profuse emotional bloodletting at the lovely house in Vernonnet — perhaps explaining Bonnard's corpse-like depictions of Marthe, in later years, as she soaked in her sarcophagus tub.

KAMAL

AJA WAS CRYING when she phoned. It was the morning after I had arrived in Paris. Liz was at a meeting.

At first, I couldn't tell if something was seriously wrong, aside from the fact that I had just spent the night with another woman. She had just gotten a call from her mother, in Mumbai: Her father had been diagnosed with pancreatic cancer and wasn't expected to live more than a month.

Aja grew hysterical, insisting that I come home that day. I tried to calm her, but she only became more agitated.

I assured her I would come back that evening.

I had booked tickets for the three of us to travel to Mumbai in August for a three-week visit. But clearly, those plans would have to change.

"Where are you right now?" She was wailing like a wounded animal.

"I'm about to go into a meeting, Aja."

"You need to be here with Yamir and me."

"I will be home this evening, Aja. I will change our tickets," I assured her. "We will leave for Mumbai in a couple of days. Begin packing. I promise you, we will get there in time for you to be with your father."

She quieted down. I could hear Yamir crying.

"We need you here," she said.

"I will be there tonight."

I clicked off and sat on Liz's bed. My eyes fixated on a poster of a Bonnard painting on the opposite wall. On the right stood a naked man. He was young and lean. The picture of virility. On the other side of the canvas was a naked woman, sitting on the bed, playing with two kittens. I ached for Liz in that moment. I would wait for her to return from her meeting. I wanted to make love to her one more time before holy hell broke loose in my life.

I called the airlines and changed our flights to Mumbai. I called Aja back. She seemed calmer.

"We will leave the day after tomorrow," I told her. "Can you be ready? Call your cousin. She can help you with Yamir and the packing."

"Yes, I can be ready," she said. "Thank you, Kamal."

"Of course, Aja. It is what we must do."

When Liz returned, I greeted her at the door and told her my bad news.

"Oh, Kamal. I'm so sorry."

"No, I'm so sorry," I said. "I will be gone for some time."

"How long?"

"A month. Maybe longer."

"What time will you leave today?"

"There's a train at six."

"What shall we do till then?" she asked.

I unbuttoned her blouse and wrapped my arms around her bare waist. I wanted to memorize every delicious curve and pastry-filled crevice of her.

Our lovemaking that afternoon was beyond what I had ever known. I wanted her in my life forever. I knew that. I was desperate to figure out a way to make that happen.

I looked at the poster on the wall opposite the bed before we said good-bye. In the center of the painting was a folded screen made of wood and cloth that separated the man from his lover. A divide was rising between Liz and me. I knew that. But I was determined to overcome it. I was not going to surrender to the miserable life that had me in its clutches.

LIZ

A FEW DAYS after Kamal returned to London, I drove to Vernonnet.

Kamal's sudden departure had left me at loose ends, especially knowing that he wouldn't be back anytime soon. I had set myself up for this, getting involved with a married man. I wondered if the distance between us would cool things off. Maybe that's just what we needed.

On the drive to Vernonnet, I let the change in scenery shift my perspective. I tried to put aside thoughts of Kamal and focus on the mission at hand.

Monsieur and Madame Lambert, the current owners of the Bonnard house, had agreed to meet with me. Their former housekeeper Sylvie Chastain was under investigation, along with a Paris art dealer named Émile Legrand, who disappeared a few weeks before the forgery charges were filed. Legrand had arranged the sale of the painting, as Sylvie's agent, and she, in turn, had paid him a very generous commission.

The Lamberts clearly were distressed by the scandal. "We had to let Sylvie go. It was a terrible situation for us," Madame

Lambert told me. "I am sure she is innocent. But there are so many unanswered questions."

I sensed there was more to what happened with Sylvie than the Lamberts shared with me that day. It was difficult for me to read them. They were polite, but reserved, obviously uncomfortable with the unwanted attention the case had brought them. Having owned a prestigious gallery before their retirement, they were part of the Paris art scene, where they were highly regarded. I could easily envision them holding court at a gallery opening. But I had a harder time imagining them in a courtroom answering pointed questions about their association with Émile Legrand and Sylvie.

The auction had taken place at Sotheby's London headquarters in March. The forgery claim was filed in June, not long after the Chinese buyer took possession of the painting. At first, Sotheby's vigorously defended the painting's authenticity, claiming it was a previously unknown Bonnard. Proving it was a fake was far more difficult than proving it was a copy of a known original.

Sylvie claimed that the painting had belonged to her late grandfather André Chastain, Bonnard's gardener. But questions quickly surfaced. How did he acquire it? Why was there no mention of it in Bonnard's journals? He typically sketched his works before he rendered them on canvas. This erotic depiction of Renée was nowhere in his sketchbooks.

But this scene of her was so *plausible* — and tantalizing, especially with Marthe in the shadows. Marthe had been relegated to a corner of *Young Women in the Garden*, where she watched a glowing Renée coquettishly capture Bonnard's attention. Placing Marthe behind the curtain in the bedroom was perversely perfect.

A key to this case would be a chemical analysis of the paint. Surely Legrand knew that would be the tripwire. But maybe all he cared about was collecting his commission. The Lamberts said Sylvie paid him 20 percent of the staggering $30 million sale price – more than enough for him to enjoy his new life in obscurity.

The Lamberts believed Legrand initially had come to neighboring Giverny, looking for Impressionist-era originals that have long been rumored to be held by private owners there. In Monet's time, when Giverny was a thriving artists' colony, paintings were used essentially as currency to pay hotel and bar bills. It's said that a young impoverished Monet, when he was living in nearby Bennecourt, had tried to pay the local butcher with a painting and threatened to throw himself in the Seine when the butcher insisted on cash instead.

Young bohemian painters from Paris, many of them American, stayed at the Hôtel Baudy for pennies a day. The proprietress, Angélina Baudy, mothered them and cooked for them and hung their paintings in the dining room and above the bar. Her makeshift gallery attracted dealers of the day. But paintings also circulated freely in the village.

"There are original works from well-known artists of that time in homes around here that museums know nothing about," Monsieur Lambert told me.

"How can that be?" It was incredible to me that these paintings could still be in hiding, in effect, after more than a century.

He shrugged. "And why not?"

Why not, indeed.

April 20

ÉMILE

As I followed Sylvie up the stairs to her bedroom that night, I wasn't ready for what was coming.

A single bulb shielded by a glass globe hung over the narrow staircase. The hallway upstairs was dark.

I carried the snifters of cognac and followed her into a bedroom. She didn't turn on the light. Instead, she went to the nightstand by the bed and lit a candle. I sensed she had planned this. But I could tell she was nervous. I saw her hand tremble as she held the match.

I handed her one of the glasses.

"To this beautiful evening," I said to her.

She smiled. We clinked and sipped. She sat down on the edge of the bed and looked up at me.

The wide bed had a canopy draped with swags of antique lace. The bedspread and decorative pillows were made of heirloom linens. An old trunk sat at the foot of the bed.

She put her glass on the nightstand. I took another swig and did the same. I shed my tie and jacket and sat down next to her. She looked lovely in the candle glow. I leaned in for a kiss. She closed her eyes, wanting it.

"Do you want to undress me?" I whispered.

"Yes."

She was adept. This wasn't an older woman uptight about sex. It was soon clear, though, that she hadn't been made love to in a while.

She climaxed quickly, during foreplay. But she came again that night. I loved giving her pleasure.

⸺

I hadn't intended to spend the night. But it was nearly daybreak when I woke up. I quietly got out of bed, careful not to wake her. She looked so peaceful in her sleep.

I wrapped a throw from the foot of the bed around me. It was then that I saw the painting, on the far wall of the room.

I moved closer, not quite believing what I was seeing. It was unmistakably in the style of Bonnard. But it was a painting I had never seen. The woman on the bed was similar to Marthe, but this woman had fuller breasts and a fleshier figure. Her facial features were distinct, unlike Bonnard's blurred renderings of Marthe. This woman was glowingly young. There was something intensely private about this moment he had captured.

"What do you think?"

Sylvie's voice startled me. I turned to see her propped up on an elbow, looking very sleepy.

"This?" I looked back at the painting.
"It's what you think."
"Where did it come from?"
"Come back to bed and I'll tell you."
And so my seduction of Sylvie became her seduction of me.

SYLVIE

As we lay in bed that morning, I told Émile the story of the painting.

Shortly after Renée committed suicide, Bonnard's new bride insisted that he destroy his paintings of his beautiful young lover.

Bonnard supposedly asked my grandfather if he would take this painting of Renée. It was his favorite of her. He was devastated by her suicide, but had to please Marthe, who wanted to be rid of Renée's memory.

The painting wasn't a gift exactly. Bonnard gave it to Papa for safekeeping, my father once told me. But Bonnard never reclaimed it.

At the outbreak of World War II, Bonnard moved with Marthe to a house he owned in Le Cannet, a village in the hills overlooking Cannes on the French Riviera. My grandfather never saw him again.

Papa always kept the painting in his bedroom at the house. He had been without a wife to keep his bed warm for many years. My grandmother had died of cancer when she was in her 40s. So the painting may have given him some comfort in his lonely nights.

Émile wanted to know if the painting had ever been exhibited.

"Never. It's our family secret."

I could tell he was intrigued. It was the first time I had ever told anyone about the painting. I kept it in my bedroom, just as my grandfather had kept it in his bedroom, so that our family secret would stay that way.

I was an only child. My parents were dead. I had no heirs, no next of kin. I knew the painting was worth a considerable amount and had always thought that one day I would sell it so that I could live comfortably in my retirement. That time would be coming soon.

When I met Émile, I saw a way to sell it. He was an art dealer with good connections. He could guide me through the process.

I broached the subject with him that morning in bed.

"Of course, Sylvie, I can help you." He kissed me. "You are full of delightful surprises." He slipped his hand between my legs.

We made love again as the room filled with the soft light of morning.

August 2015

KAMAL

AJA'S FATHER DIED two weeks after we arrived in Mumbai.

It was a stressful time for everyone. Her mother went to pieces. Her three sisters did, too. The only sane one in the bunch was Aja's only brother, the eldest sibling. He was poised to take over as the family patriarch. I'd always liked Seth and was secretly glad it was he, not I, who had to take charge of this family of wailing women.

Aja projected stoicism, for her mother's sake. But when she was alone with me, she unleashed her grief – and anger. I was to blame that our life together had taken her away from her family.

"You didn't have to marry me," I yelled at her one night. I had never raised my voice to her. I could see the shock on her face. She was standing by the bed in our secluded garden cottage, behind her parents' house.

"I know you don't love me," she said.

"You never gave me a chance." My rage, too, was roiling. "You play the victim in this marriage. But you have inflicted great pain, Aja. You're a heartless woman."

"Get out!" She pointed to the door. "I don't want you in my bed."

I was stunned. But part of me was relieved. "You want me out of your life, too?" I desperately wanted her to say yes.

"That's what you want, isn't it? So you can go to Paris to be with your mistress."

"Yes, that's exactly what I want."

I regretted those words the moment I said them. But I was beyond caring about consequences. I knew I had set in motion a maelstrom of heartache and torment. But I truly didn't care.

LIZ

KAMAL CALLED ME from Mumbai one night. He sounded drunk. I couldn't catch everything he was saying. There was a lot of background noise.

"Where are you?" I asked.

"The airport."

"Where are you going?"

"Paris."

"What?"

"I can't stand another day away from you. I'm coming to Paris." His speech was slurred. "Fuck 'em. I don't give a bloody fuck anymore."

"Kamal. What's happened?"

"I don't give a fuck anymore. Do you understand me, Liz? Please say you do."

"Oh, Kamal."

"I've had too much to drink. Can you tell?"

"Yes."

"Do you hate me for being this way?"

"No."

"Do you love me?" He was quiet for a moment. "I love you."

I didn't want to have this conversation, not with him ten sheets to the wind.

"I want us to tell each other these things in person. Not like this."

"I need to hear you say you love me." He sounded like he was on the verge of tears.

"Kamal, listen to me. Get yourself some coffee and then get yourself on that plane, ok?"

"Liz, I love you."

I gave in. "I love you, too, Kamal."

"I'm happy now. I'm so happy, Liz." He started to cry.

My heart ached. "Kamal...what time do you get to Paris?"

"In the day time. I can't remember exactly."

"Kamal, I'm here. Call me when you arrive in Paris, ok?"

"Ok. I love you."

He clicked off.

I sat on my bed looking at the print of the naked man and his mistress — Bonnard and Marthe — feeling like I was sinking into a dark, unforgiving place.

⁂

The next morning, I went out for groceries. Many stores and restaurants in the neighborhood were closed, as is typical of Paris in August.

I was glad to see the little deli-market on the corner was open. The owner was an older Kurdish man named Asan. I was in the habit of stopping by the shop each day to say hello and pick up a few things. Asan was always welcoming and cheerful. His nephew, Tomar, who looked to be in his late teens, worked behind the counter, making sandwiches. Asan told me Tomar had come to live with him after his parents died in a U.S. bombing of Iraq when Tomar was a child.

Tomar was there that day, but not Asan. He was shy and awkward, not chatty like his uncle. He wasn't used to working the register and seemed flustered as he rang up my purchases: baguettes, jam, eggs and cheese for an omelet, and freshly ground coffee. Kamal was going to need lots of coffee. Or maybe he just needed to sleep it off.

Kamal called early that afternoon.

"I'm in the taxi queue." He sounded groggy.

"At Charles de Gaulle?"

"Yes. I'll be there soon."

"I love you, Kamal."

"I love you, too." He sounded exhausted.

When Kamal appeared at my door that afternoon, he looked like a broken man. He had lost some weight and had dark circles under his eyes.

He folded me in his arms. We stood like that for a few minutes. I felt like I was holding him up.

This wasn't the man full of passion who had shared my bed only a few weeks earlier. This was a soldier home from an emotionally devastating war.

The story poured out of him as we lay in that bed together.

"Aja immediately went to my father and told him she wanted a divorce. She told him I had been unfaithful. That I had a mistress in Paris. And probably others. She didn't know how many. She feared for her health. *Her health*." I could see his anger rising. "Even if I had sexual diseases, she wouldn't catch them from me. She never let me near her.

"My father was enraged, of course. I had gone out that night, after my argument with her, to a bar in Mumbai. When I came back, it was very late. I went home to my parents' house, which is just down the road from where Aja's family lives, not knowing Aja had been there earlier that evening. My father was waiting for me. Like a jackal waiting to pounce."

Kamal closed his eyes. He was struggling to keep his emotions in check. I put my hand on his bare chest and he held it tight.

"It was a horrible argument. At one point, he lunged at me and tried to push me down the porch steps. He refused to let me in the house."

He squeezed my hand tighter.

"He told me Aja would file for divorce. He assured me she would get sole custody of Yamir. And then he told me to leave. *I never want to see you again*, he said."

"What did you do?"

"What could I do? I called a taxi and went to a hotel."

"Kamal, I'm so sorry."

I stroked his cheek as he closed his eyes. Within a few minutes, he was asleep.

It was about nine that night when Kamal woke up. I could see him stirring from where I was sitting on the sofa. I put down my book and went to him and crawled into bed beside him.

He smiled at me.

"A smile," I said, tracing the outline of his lips with my finger.

"I'm here with you. Good reason to smile."

He kissed me gently. Everything was gentle about our lovemaking that night. A page had turned. It was a new beginning for us. This was no longer a passionate fling born of a random encounter. We had chosen this path, for better or for worse.

September 2014

ÉMILE

AFTER SYLVIE'S BIG reveal, I made frequent trips to Giverny during the next several months. I couldn't believe my good fortune. The sale of her Bonnard would fatten my wallet. But I also was grateful to have Sylvie in my life. I enjoyed her company. She was an intelligent, attractive woman who appreciated fine art. We were a good fit.

She didn't want to part with the Bonnard. I knew that. But she needed the money. I started making inquiries about what the painting might fetch at auction. There was immediate interest. An unknown Bonnard could sell for millions of dollars. But a painting of the infamously tragic Renée could send the price through the roof.

I explained to Sylvie that the painting would need to be authenticated. I contacted Sotheby's in London. They were eager to see it. We set a date for Sotheby's agents to come to the house. Two curators from the Orsay were there as well.

I could tell Sylvie was uneasy that morning. It was then that I understood how conflicted she was about letting the painting go. There was great excitement in the group. I wondered if the Orsay might get into the bidding war.

But I could tell Sylvie was having second thoughts. After everyone left, she burst into tears.

"What's wrong, *chérie*? I thought you'd be delighted."

"I know I should be happy. But I feel like I'm selling a part of me."

She stood looking at the painting. I stepped behind her, with my arms around her waist.

"She will always be a part of you."

August 2015

LIZ

The results of the paint analysis confirmed *Renée* was a fake. The forger had tried to mix something with the pigments to fool the lab geeks, but science had outmatched connivery.

The story made headlines. Sotheby's defense crumbled. They were on the hook for $30 million. I assumed they'd go after Sylvie Chastain to recover the sale proceeds. But she had already paid a $6 million commission to Legrand, who had disappeared without a trace.

A warrant was issued for Legrand's arrest. His disappearance cast a long shadow over Sylvie Chastain as well.

She had been seen with Legrand on a number of occasions in Giverny. They appeared to have been romantically involved. She claimed she had entrusted Legrand with the arrangements for the auction and that it was her belief, based on documentation from Sotheby's and the Orsay curators, that the painting was authentic.

The Orsay was cooperating with the investigation, mostly in defense of its reputation. Although my work for Sotheby's was finished, the Orsay hired me as a consultant while the criminal investigation continued. My relationship with Sotheby's had become strained. After all, I had ordered the paint-sample test that had destroyed their case. In a heated phone conversation with a Sotheby's agent, I pointedly questioned their lack of due diligence.

The case took an interesting turn. Investigators called me in, along with a Bonnard expert from the Orsay. The question they put to us: Was the auctioned painting a blatant fraud or was it a copy of a Bonnard original? The Orsay's Bonnard expert and I had had lengthy discussions about this. Given what we both knew about Bonnard's sordid private life and the woman's striking resemblance to his other depictions of Renée, we were inclined to think it was a well-executed copy. Which, of course, presented a different mystery: Where was the original?

One night, I projected the photos Sotheby's took in Sylvie's bedroom, onto a wall underneath the skylight of my apartment.

In the moonlight that night, the projection of the painting took on an ethereal quality. This was a scene of Renée in the seductive darkness of night. Her skin is bathed in candle glow. The sheet covering the mattress ripples around her body. Marthe, peering from behind the curtain, looked even creepier hovering on the wall than she did on my Mac screen.

And then I projected the images taken in London. There was something dissimilar about them. The difference in lighting could have accounted for this. The photos taken in

Sylvie Chastain's bedroom had a more intimate feeling than those shot for Sotheby's catalog in a well-lit professional studio.

But it was more than that. I couldn't help but feel a major clue in this mystery was right before my eyes.

September 2014

SYLVIE

IT WAS MY habit every night to take a candlelight bath in the tub that had once been Marthe's.

I could understand why my grandfather would have been pleased to take this bathtub when Bonnard left Vernonnet. My grandmother had been in poor health long before her cancer was diagnosed. My father said Papa used to pour warm baths for her in Marthe's tub and float flowers in the water, which he would mix with soothing salts.

My grandfather was a sturdy, hardworking man. But he also was a tenderhearted romantic who revered beauty. His gardening style reflected that. He knew how to bend and peg a rose cane so that a bud would form at every notch. I remember an archway he created from rose canes in our own garden that took my breath away.

I think that Papa would have felt great sympathy for Marthe. He likened her to a bird with a broken wing. She won Bonnard in the end, but her spirit was permanently crippled by his affair with Renée.

The first time Émile spent the night with me, he was stunned by the painting – and also, the tub, when I told him it had been Marthe's. It had featured in so many of Bonnard's paintings of her that it was an *objet d'art* in its own right.

Many an evening, Émile and I would soak in the tub together. We just fit, with me leaning back against him, snugly between his legs.

Those few months of spring were the happiest of my life. I had found a man who truly loved me and wanted nothing but my happiness. We spoke of the life we would have together after the painting sold. I would quit my job. We would travel together. We made a list of places we wanted to visit: the Galapagos Islands, India, the Outback of Australia.

"What about Tahiti?" he asked me one night in the tub. He was massaging my breasts with a soapy sponge.

My eyes were closed. I imagined a beach of white soft sand rimming an aqua lagoon and heard palm fronds rustling in the breeze.

"We could see where Paul Gauguin lived," he said. "He had a big influence on Bonnard."

I loved Gauguin's portraits of Polynesian women, surrounded by exotic tropical plants, all painted in vibrantly exciting colors.

"Yes to Tahiti." I smiled. "Yes to everything."

"To this?" he asked, as he moved his hand lower.

"Everything."

September 2015

LIZ

KAMAL STAYED WITH me in Paris into September. He needed to go to London for a few days and invited me to come with him.

Aja had insisted that he ship her clothing and her family heirlooms to Mumbai. "She wants everything in the kitchen, the artwork, the furnishings. She wants Yamir's toys sent by express courier – not in the shipping container. She says he misses his Duplos." Kamal ran his hands through his hair while reading her e-mail as we sat at the kitchen table of his Chelsea townhouse. "Why can't someone go buy him a goddamn bucket of Duplos?"

I was worried about Kamal. He wasn't sleeping well. He looked like hell. He had lost more weight since he'd come back to Paris, despite my efforts to fatten him with buttery croissants and my homemade crème brûlée.

In his sleep-deprived state, he was often short-tempered. He didn't lash out at me, but he was annoyed at the world. Every time an e-mail came from Aja, I could see the tension rise in him. When e-mails from her lawyers were in the mix, he would sometimes go into a rage. One day, he smashed a glass in my kitchen sink and cut his hand, leaving blood on the floor.

I soothed him with sex. We had sex every day, sometimes twice a day. He'd sleep a little after, but it wasn't restful sleep.

I suggested he see a therapist. He resisted at first. But when we were in London, he called a friend who gave him the name of someone he could contact.

"Would you like me to go with you?" I asked him.

"No, my darling. I don't want to drag you into this."

"You're not dragging me into anything. I want to help you feel better."

"I know, Liz. I love you for that. Truly, I do. I know how hard this is for you."

―

Kamal's home was beautifully decorated with exotic pieces from India and his world travels. He and Aja came from money, that was clear. He had made his own fortune, but he was worried about the cost of the divorce and the support payments Aja would demand. His father was writing him vicious e-mails, berating him and vowing that Kamal would never see Yamir again.

"I can live with this," Kamal said to me as we packed up Yamir's toys one afternoon. "But never seeing my son again is unthinkable." He picked up a photo of Yamir that was sitting on the dresser. "I don't care what Aja says. These photos are mine."

Kamal hired his own attorneys, and the money-sucking battle began. He had no hope of winning. I knew that. I'm sure he knew that. Aja was back at base camp, surrounded by family and a war chest of funds and legal support.

I saw Kamal sinking deeper and I didn't know how to help him.

―⸺

The criminal investigation continued as the search for Émile Legrand escalated. The Orsay had aggressively stepped up to substantiate its claim that the painting their curators had seen at Sylvie Chastain's residence was an original. I had a front row seat to this debate that involved some of the leading experts of Post-Impressionist French art.

Then came the shocking news: Sylvie Chastain had attempted suicide at her house in Giverny. She had been found bleeding from the wrists, in her Marthe de Méligny bathtub.

KAMAL

I KNEW I was worrying Liz. I finally promised her I'd get myself into therapy. I wanted to assure her I wasn't losing it. But I wasn't convinced myself.

I started making weekly trips to London. Tuesday to Friday. Soon I was seeing my therapist there twice a week.

The sessions were rough at first. I was dredging up years and years of family shit. Beneath it all was my suppressed outrage at the marriage that had been forced upon me. I hated my father. I hated Aja's father. I hated Aja for her spinelessness.

I was teetering at the edge of the abyss. My business was tanking. I assured myself I could stay afloat, at least for a while, if I sold the townhouse.

But then what?

Liz would be heading back to the U.S. eventually. I knew her work in Paris was only temporary. I had nothing tangible to offer her.

When I was in Paris with her, I longed for her to lead me to her bed. She was my painkiller of choice.

The only solace I knew happened during our lovemaking. I escaped to a place of euphoria, but just for a short while. And then I was back in the depths of my hell on earth.

LIZ

Sylvie Chastain's attempted suicide threw the investigation into a tailspin. Did she try to kill herself because she was Legrand's accomplice and now fearful she'd be spending her retirement in jail? Or did she slit her wrists in despair? She had a painting worth nothing and apparently had fallen for a shyster agent who had convinced her he loved her and would make her rich.

After she was discharged from the hospital, Sylvie went into seclusion at an unknown locale. The media caught scent of her trail and soon found out she was holed up at her lawyer's estate, near Versailles.

I wondered how she could afford an attorney who had an estate near Versailles.

"She can't," Detective Hobbs told me, as we sat in his makeshift office at the Orsay one afternoon. "He's in it for the publicity."

A British forgery specialist from Scotland Yard, Hobbs was a jolly, rotund guy, 50ish, with a nose for stinky fish. I had worked with him on other cases, including one a few years earlier involving a fake Gainsborough that went up for auction at an English estate-liquidation sale. The forger had died years ago, so there were no criminal charges to be filed. The family was devastated about losing out on a tidy sum they had been banking on, but kept stiff upper lips. Privately, they were embarrassed they had naively believed they were owners of an heirloom masterwork. Hobbs and I had had a good laugh about it over a couple of pints at the local pub. It was a really bad fake.

But this case had us both stymied.

"What's your best theory about what's happened here?" I asked him. "Do you think Legrand knew about the painting and seduced her to get it?"

"Not necessarily. I think he was snooping around Giverny, hoping to uncover something." Hobbs sat back in his chair and folded his hands on his chest. "I think he knew about Sylvie's family."

"That her grandfather had a connection to Bonnard?"

"Sure. That wasn't a big secret. Legrand purposely went to her looking for a way in. Giverny is a small village. The residents don't welcome outsiders. The garden walls are high there, for good reason. He wanted access and Sylvie could help him with that."

"So he got lucky?"

"If you believe Sylvie had a genuine Bonnard."

I smiled, knowing what was coming next. Invariably when I worked on cases with Hobbs, he'd push aside every hunch and piece of evidence and start from scratch.

"How do we know Sylvie's story – about Bonnard giving the painting to her grandfather – is true?" he asked, playing devil's advocate.

"You think she bought a fake Bonnard at a flea market and was trying to hoodwink Legrand, Sotheby's and the Orsay?"

Hobbs chuckled. "But do you think it's strange that Bonnard gave the painting to his gardener?"

"Bonnard wasn't a straight arrow, as we know," I said. "He had two mistresses. He lied to Marthe at every turn, even after Renée's death. He kept paintings of Renée, but apparently told Marthe he had destroyed them. That one of the two women in the garden, for example, with Miss Renée Sunshine front and center and Marthe looking at her from the corner of the painting. He hid that one away somewhere. After Marthe died, he re-worked it and changed Renée from a brunette to a blonde. He was an old man then – what, in his 70s? Why would he do that? He was possessed by an obsession."

Hobbs pondered a photocopy of Bonnard's nude Renée, pinned to the wall above his desk. "This may well be the painting he prized the most. He gave it to the gardener for safekeeping. I get that." He clicked open a file on his computer screen. "So how do we explain this damning lab report of yours? Clearly, the chemical analysis proves there's an additive in the paint mix that wasn't available in Bonnard's time."

"Bait-and-switch," I said matter-of-factly. "Yes, the painting that was auctioned at Sotheby's was a fake. But the painting that Sotheby's saw in her bedroom was an original."

"How do you propose we prove that, Sherlock?"

"My dear, Watson, there's nothing more deceptive than an obvious fact." I grinned at him. "Let's take another look at the photos."

September 2014

ÉMILE

Sylvie had lingered in the tub that night, after we had talked about where our travels would take us. Our foreplay usually started in Marthe's tub. That night, Sylvie was enjoying the aftereffect of an intense orgasm.

I sat in the candle glow of the bedroom, looking at Renée on the wall. She, too, had the look of a woman satiated by sex, but still wanting more.

I pulled my phone out of my jacket pocket and took a few photos, zooming in for a close-up of Bonnard's signature. I had no doubt this painting was going to create a huge buzz in the art world.

Sylvie came into the room, wrapped in her fluffy robe, as I scrolled through the photos.

"I want to bring a colleague of mine here next week. He'd like to see her before she goes to London. Would that be okay?"

"Fine." She crawled onto the bed and wrapped her arms around me.

"How are you feeling about all this?" I turned to her.

"Hot," she whispered, kissing my neck.

I smiled as I lay back on the bed. She took off her robe. Her flushed damp skin shone in the candlelight. She looked so young in that moment. I easily could imagine her at Renée's age.

But Sylvie wasn't an innocent ingénue. She knew how to give a man pleasure. I loved that she had no inhibitions with me.

She mounted me and slowly brought me to a climax. She came, too, again.

As we lay in each other's arms that night, I couldn't imagine life without her. I understood the hold Renée must have had on Bonnard. But I couldn't fathom Bonnard's fiendish pleasure, living with two lovers – one in the next room as he made love to the other. Evidently, it heightened his warped sexual excitement, envisioning Marthe's jealously as she venomously peered at her much younger rival from behind a curtain.

I closed my mind to that thought. I had Sylvie, and she was more than enough.

September 2015

LIZ

NOT LONG AFTER Sylvie Chastain's suicide attempt, Hobbs asked me to attend a meeting in London, at Scotland Yard.

Kamal was spending a few days each week in London and weekends with me in Paris. Of course, he welcomed my impromptu visit.

I liked seeing Kamal in his home environment. He seemed more anchored and focused there. I sensed his therapy sessions were helping him. Despite his anger over the divorce proceedings that were costing him a small fortune, he had resigned himself to the outcome and was looking forward to our future together.

Although Kamal had made quick work of clearing the house of Aja's things, I still sensed her presence there. I was grateful Kamal and I didn't sleep in their bed. On my first visit to the house a couple of weeks earlier, he kindly had said to me, "I think we'll be more comfortable in the guestroom." I had appreciated that. I couldn't help but think of Bonnard's ghostly Marthe.

I was up early on the morning of the meeting, reviewing my notes about the case. I had never been to Scotland Yard. Most of my meetings took place at museums, galleries and auction houses, not at world-famous police compounds. In my active imagination, I wondered if Hobbs was going to present us with a lineup of forgery suspects.

"Are you on the verge of a breakthrough in the case?" Kamal asked at breakfast.

I smiled as he slathered jam on his toast, remembering our first breakfast together in Provence. He was gaining back his lost weight. I loved watching him lick jam off his thumb as he devoured that piece of toast.

"I'm not sure. But there must be some reason why Hobbs has called in the troops."

In fact, Hobbs had arranged a meeting that morning with the entire investigation team. Scotland Yard had been tracking the painting's whereabouts once it had entered the U.K. On the French side, security at Charles de Gaulle had followed the painting's path through the airport and had questioned the courier agents. Everything checked out. All the log sheets. The surveillance videos. Nothing appeared to be out of line.

As the morning meeting adjourned, I wondered why he had brought us to the table when there appeared to be no new information to consider.

Hobbs pulled me aside and quietly asked me to join him for lunch.

Once we were outside, he said, "I didn't want to say anything in front of the others. Not yet."

"You're killin' me, Hobbs."

He smiled. I could tell he was on to something.

Hobbs took me to the Sherlock Holmes Pub around the corner from his office.

"I love the venue," I said as we sat down at a booth in the back.

"I come here for inspiration." Hobbs smiled, pointing to a display above the bar of an animal's footprint in a glass-encased slab of mud.

I laughed. "Clearly, the imprint of a Baskerville hound." A plaster-of-paris hound's head hung next to the glass case.

We ordered Ploughman's lunches and pints of lager. True to form, Hobbs quickly got down to business.

"I've been thinking about what you said — about the photos. I've had them enhanced," he said.

"Has something caught your eye?"

"I see what you mean about the difference in the two sets. The ones taken in Sylvie Chastain's bedroom are probably truer to Bonnard's palette."

"Most likely. The lighting in Sotheby's London studio was much more intense."

"But the subdued lighting in the bedroom could have masked some obscure nuances of the painting that a photograph might miss. Also, we need to consider that the painting could have darkened a bit with time. It probably had never been properly cleaned."

"What are you suggesting?"

"What if a forger worked from photographs and never saw the original? What might have been lost in the digital images?"

"Subtleties in shading," I said. "Color hues might be lost.

The waitress set our pints on the table. Hobbs raised his glass and said with a wink, "You need to look at something."

⁓

I couldn't wait to get back to his office.

"You didn't have to inhale your lunch," he teased me as we walked back from the pub.

"You've whetted my appetite for a bigger feast."

Hobbs took me into a projection room, down the hall from his office, with a large screen – a better backdrop than the cracked, whitewashed walls of my Paris apartment.

"Make yourself comfortable," he said.

I took a seat next to him, at a table where he set up his laptop. He dimmed the lights and started the slideshow.

"These first images are the ones that the Sotheby's agent took the day they were at the house to authenticate the painting."

I knew those images well.

"Now...these are the same photos, but our lab played with the exposure on this one...and the contrast on this one."

Nothing popped out at me.

"But watch what happens here when I zoom in," he said.

An enlarged image of Renée's crotch appeared on the screen.

"Hello!" I exclaimed with a laugh.

"I don't mean to offend," Hobbs apologized. "But look carefully here...just below."

He clicked through a few images, enhanced to show the subtle coloration of the sheet underneath her.

"My god." I couldn't believe what I was seeing.

"Evidence of his virgin conquest, I'd say."

On the sheet beneath her was a smudge of blood.

Hobbs clicked to another slide. "This is a photo taken at Sotheby's in London. The studio lighting is much stronger, so the stain should be more noticeable."

But the sheet was clean.

I looked at Hobbs. "Somewhere between Giverny and London, her bedding accidentally went through the laundry."

He smirked. "The forger's mistake."

September 2014

SYLVIE

ÉMILE BROUGHT HIS colleague to the house. His name was Paul. I didn't catch his last name. He was a nervous chain smoker with blond hair and ice-blue eyes.

Paul was knowledgeable about Bonnard's work. Émile said Paul had worked for him for many years as an appraiser. Paul asked if he could photograph the painting. I said of course.

Paul took many photos that day. He seemed particularly interested in Bonnard's signature.

I asked Émile to step into the hallway. "Is there a problem, Émile?"

"No, no, *chérie*. I just want Paul's opinion."

"Do you have doubts?"

"I have no doubts. I assure you. I just want documentation. This is a previously unknown painting entering the world art market. I don't want anyone claiming it's a fake."

"But Sotheby's and the Orsay are convinced."

"I'm convinced, too. I just want these photos for our archives. This is our only chance to do this."

I studied his face.

"Are you okay with this?" he asked

"Selling the painting, you mean?"

He nodded. "Tell me now. We can still stop this."

"I must sell. There's no other way."

"It will be fine, Sylvie. You'll see. We have each other and a wonderful life ahead of us."

And then he kissed me.

I trusted Émile completely.

September 2015

LIZ

After I saw Hobbs' slideshow, he reconvened the meeting that afternoon, with a shift in his agenda.

"I'm working on a new hunch, based on some enhanced images of the painting," he told the group. "I've seen the statements from Sotheby's packing agents. Were any photos taken of the painting that day, when the painting was crated?"

A French detective on the case looked through his files. "No. There were no photos taken on the day the packers came."

"Is that usual?" Hobbs turned to an older British gentleman, a senior director from Sotheby's London office.

"Our agent arrived late that morning," he said. "She got lost on her way to Giverny. The packers had already wrapped the painting by the time she got there."

Hobbs rolled his eyes. "Would it be your expectation that she should have photographed the painting before it was crated, if she had arrived on time?"

"Yes, that would have been my expectation."

"So it seems to me that Sotheby's has fallen down twice here." Hobbs could look like a bulldog when his temper flared. "You failed to do a paint analysis that would have told you that the painting was a forgery. You had it at your disposal in London for four months before the auction. And you failed to photograph the painting on the day of shipment. A switch could have happened before it left Giverny."

A murmur went around the table.

I smiled. Hobbs smelled stinky fish.

"I don't yet have an explanation for how this happened." Hobbs said. "My theory would suggest there is an original *Renée* out there somewhere." He thumped his fingers on the thick stack of papers in front of him. "But I think our focus should be on Sylvie Chastain. I sense she's not an innocent in all this."

September 2014

ÉMILE

THE PHOTOS PAUL had printed were strewn on my desk.

"They're much clearer on my Mac's retina display," Paul said.

"What do you think?" I asked him.

"Yes. Definitely, we can do this."

"How long before you know for sure?"

"I know now."

"I want proof." I knew Paul could promise the sky and moon. But he had fallen short before.

"You doubt me?" He was getting testy, which was always a problem with him. "When do you need *proof*?"

"In two weeks. No more."

He nodded. "You'll have what you need."

I held up Paul's photo of Bonnard's signature. "You're sure of this?"

"I have no doubt."

"Two weeks," I repeated.

"You have my promise."

September 2015

LIZ

Hobbs wanted me to come with him the day he questioned Sylvie Chastain at her attorney's estate.

"I'm not a detective. Why do you want me there?"

"You're a woman. You'll know immediately if she's lying." That made me laugh.

We pulled up at the front gate where there were several press photographers, who snapped photos of our car.

"Glad the glass is tinted," I said. One photographer had his lens a few inches from my window.

Sylvie and her attorney were waiting for us in the drawing room, decorated with gorgeous Persian rugs, antique furniture and a Gustav Klimt painting that hung above the fireplace mantel.

The attorney immediately wanted to know who I was.

"She's assisting me," Hobbs said.

"Does she have a name?" he asked.

"Liz, give him your card." Hobbs didn't go in for introductions and pleasantries.

I produced my card, which momentarily placated the attorney.

Hobbs didn't waste a minute. "Madame Chastain, may I look at your wrists?"

The attorney quickly protested.

"Save your objections for the courtroom," Hobbs told him.

Sylvie put out her wrists, bottom side down.

"Turn them over, please," Hobbs instructed her.

She obliged. He leaned over to take a closer look. From where I was sitting, I couldn't see what he was looking at.

He sat down next to her and made a note on a pad he took from his pocket. He looked at her for a moment and then asked, "Why did you try to kill yourself?"

Sylvie teared up and couldn't speak for a moment. "My life is ruined."

"Why do you think so?" Hobbs asked.

"I've lost everything."

"Were you in love with Émile Legrand?"

"At the beginning, yes. Or at least I thought I was."

"Perhaps you were so taken by his charm that you didn't see what was coming?"

Sylvie bristled. "Of course I didn't see what was coming. He's a clever, devious man."

Hobbs wisely switched tacks. "Are you in the habit of locking up your house when you're not home?"

"Yes."

"Did Legrand have a key?"

"Not to my knowledge."

"Wouldn't you remember if you had given him one?"

"There was an extra key that I kept by the back door."

"Could he have taken it without your knowledge?"

"Possibly. It's not something I would notice immediately, unless I needed to use it."

"Do you think he could have switched the paintings when you weren't home? Maybe one day when you were at work?"

She hesitated. "I hadn't considered that."

"Really?"

"You don't believe me?" She looked at her attorney and asked, "Does he think I'm lying?" She shook her head. "This is all too much." And then she started to cry.

Her attorney squared off with Hobbs. "Enough. It's clear Madame Chastain is still recovering from severe trauma. This meeting is over."

Hobbs jotted something on his notepad and stood up. "No harm intended. Thank you for allowing us to visit."

Hobbs turned to Sylvie. "Madame Chastain..." She didn't acknowledge him. "I hope you're feeling better soon."

And with that, we left.

"That seemed a waste of time," I said when we were back in the car.

"Not at all, Sherlock," Hobbs said.

"What did I miss?"

"According to the police, the spare key was on the hook by the back door – with Legrand's fingerprints on it."

"But that doesn't prove she knew about the switch."

Hobbs smiled at me. "Those wrist cuts were nothing but scratches."

"Meaning?"

"I think she faked her suicide attempt."

KAMAL

Finally, a month after I had returned from Mumbai, Aja agreed to let me skype with Yamir. This was a major breakthrough in the blackout she had imposed at the beginning. But Yamir was a strong-willed child, who was missing his father. She had finally relented.

It cut me to the core to see him so far away and not be able to hold him on my lap. Although I had been a miserable husband, I had been a good father. I had looked forward to being a dad in all the stages of Yamir's life.

He was elated to see me the first time we skyped. "Daddy! Daddy!" He turned to Aja who was off-camera. "Look, Mama, it's Daddy."

He showed me an action figure he had gotten. It looked like Batman. And then he showed me a little painting he had done at school of his family. "That's you, Daddy," he said, pointing to a man holding a briefcase who stood at the edge of the picture, far from the house where his mama stood at the doorway.

"I miss you, Daddy," he said.

"I miss you, too, Yamir."

"When are you coming home?"

What could I say?

Aja said to him, "Come, Yamir. It's time for your supper."

"When is Daddy coming home?" he asked her.

Aja picked him up and glanced at the screen. I could see the pain in her eyes. She quickly ended the call.

I hate the feeling when you get blipped off on skype, before you've even had a chance to say a proper good-bye.

LIZ

A FEW DAYS after our session with Sylvie Chastain, Hobbs invited me to a meeting with the Lamberts at their house in Vernonnet.

His car had a screwy GPS system that kept trying to send us to Belgium. He quickly appointed me as the navigator.

"So what can you tell me about the Lamberts?" he asked as we got off the autoroute onto a winding road through Normandy's hay fields and cow pastures. "Did they tell you any juicy stories?"

"About Marthe and Renée? No." I laughed. "Madame Lambert has decorated the house in keeping with Bonnard's style. She has photos of the place when he lived there. The furnishings are authentic to the period. The day I was there, she had staged a table to look like one of his paintings – with a linen cloth and a vase of flowers. His paintings come to life everywhere you look there."

"Did they talk about Sylvie?"

"Yes, briefly. Madame Lambert said she was sad they had to let Sylvie go when the scandal broke about the forgery. I sensed she wanted to say more, but she didn't."

"What about Legrand? Did they say anything about him?"

"We didn't go there. They seemed uncomfortable. I'm not the police. I didn't feel I should question them about that." I smiled at Hobbs. "That's your job."

Our visit that morning with the Lamberts was pleasant. Madame Lambert cordially served tea and showed us a beautiful book of Bonnard's artwork that included paintings he had done in the room where we were sitting. Bonnard called the house Ma Roulotte – my caravan – because of its long, narrow floor plan. I tried to imagine him and his two women in such close proximity. The small rooms offered little privacy for intimate encounters.

Monsieur Lambert didn't say much. I'm sure he saw nothing enjoyable about having tea with a Scotland Yard detective and an American forgery expert.

At one point, Hobbs asked him, "How is it that you know Émile Legrand?"

Monsieur Lambert shrugged. "We don't know him really. He came to one of our parties."

"When was that?" Hobbs asked.

"*Je ne sais pas.* We have many parties." He looked at his wife. "Do you remember?"

Madame Lambert smoothed the napkin on her lap. "He was here twice, actually. The first time, we were away – Sylvie was here and showed him around."

Hobbs got out his notepad. "Do you remember the date of that visit?"

"I can check my book. It was March of last year, as I recall." She turned to her husband. "Remember, we were in Brittany."

Monsieur Lambert nodded.

"Did Sylvie say anything about his visit?" Hobbs asked.

Madame Lambert fingered the handle of her teacup. "She said he was charming and very interested in the story of the house. That's all."

"What was the purpose of his visit?"

"A friend of ours in Giverny knew him and suggested he come see the house. Apparently, he was working on an exhibit at the museum there and wanted to see some of the local historical sights."

Hobbs scribbled on his pad. "Were you aware that, after that meeting, Sylvie had been seen with him in Giverny on several occasions at what have been described as 'romantic' dinners?"

Madame Lambert smiled. "Yes, I had heard this. I never discussed her personal life with her, though."

"Do you have reason to think Sylvie knew Legrand before he visited here last March?"

"I don't know that to be true." Madame Lambert seemed puzzled by the question. "She never indicated that. I was under the impression she met him here."

"You said there was a second time he came to the house?" Hobbs looked up from his notepad.

Madame Lambert glanced at her husband. "Yes. We had a dinner party in the fall. He came to that."

"When exactly?"

"October. Again, I must look at my book to give you the exact date."

"Tell me about the party."

"We have dinner parties often. That one was for a group of museum donors."

"Why was Legrand invited?"

"His name was on the guest list I received from the museum."

"Was there anything memorable about him that evening?"

"Only that he arrived late." Madame Lambert sipped her tea, then said, "Sylvie seemed agitated."

"Sylvie was here?"

"Yes. She always helped with our parties."

"What happened when Émile arrived?"

"She went outside to greet him as soon as he came through the gate."

"And?" Hobbs looked at her intently.

"I was standing here on the balcony and had a good view of them." Madame Lambert gazed out the window toward the gate. "I heard him say, *It's done.*"

September 2014

ÉMILE

S*ylvie* *and* I had our first row when I told her of my plan. Actually, it was an eruption that nearly ended our relationship.

We were in bed. She was a little drunk. I had given her a generous pour of cognac that night.

"I want to talk to you about something," I said, stroking her shoulder.

"Hmmm. " She was half asleep.

I laid it all out for her. How it would happen. Why it was a perfect plan.

She suddenly was wide-awake, looking at me in disbelief. She pushed me away. "You're here in this bed because you want *her?*" She pointed at Renée.

"Don't be crazy, Sylvie. I want *you*."

"You're the one who's crazy." She sat up, holding the sheet around her. "We could go to jail for this, you know. Or is it me you want to put in jail?"

"We would do this together, *chérie*. I want us to be together always."

"Get out," she said.

"Sylvie!"

"You heard me. Get out of my sight." She slapped me across the face. "Now!" she shrieked.

I quickly got dressed and gathered my things. She sat sobbing on the bed. I turned at the bedroom door to look at her.

She threw the empty cognac snifter at me. I dodged it, but the glass shattered against the door frame.

"*Get out!*"

September 2015

LIZ

AFTER HOBBS AND I had tea with the Lamberts, we headed down the road to Giverny.

"We're meeting an investigator at Sylvie's house," Hobbs said.

"I feel like I'm in a police drama."

Hobbs chuckled. "Who knows. We could end up with our own reality TV show."

The detective was already there when we arrived. The property had been cordoned off with yellow tape. We parked in the back next to his car.

His name was Renard. He reminded me a little of Peter Sellers' Clouseau in *The Pink Panther*. He had a thin, dark moustache and a nervous twitch that caused him to blink a lot.

"*Enchanté, Mademoiselle Jennings.*" He nodded graciously as he shook my hand.

He greeted Hobbs like an old friend. They apparently had a long history of working on cases together. Over the years, Hobbs' forgery work had often brought him to Paris, where Renard had pounded the pavement as a young detective.

Renard led us through the rear garden. He opened the door with a master key for the new door locks, which had been fabricated at the police lab, he told us.

"Does this mean she can't come back here?"

"She can come back," Renard said, his eyes twinkling. "But she can't get inside."

I stifled a giggle.

I loved the kitchen, with its delft tiles and copper pots hanging above the stove. We walked through the adjacent dining area, its corner cabinets filled with lovely china and glassware. The front sitting room held a sofa with plump cushions and poufy needlepoint pillows. The large windows were draped with exquisite French lace curtains. It was easy to see Sylvie was a romantic who appreciated beautiful things.

Hobbs and I followed Renard up the narrow staircase. There were two rooms upstairs joined by a bathroom, situated end-to-end along a long hallway. One room was a study, with a desk, a daybed and bookshelves. The other was Sylvie's bedroom.

Renard put on latex gloves and raised the bedroom window blinds. Hobbs immediately went to the wall opposite the bed and inspected a rectangular discoloration on the floral wallpaper.

Before he could say anything, Renard noted, "The measurement of this rectangle matches the forgery exactly."

"The backing of the painting and the frame?" Hobbs asked.

"Both appear to be of the time period, not new. But expert forgers are good at that." Renard motioned to us. "Come see this."

He opened the door to the bathroom, which had been left untouched since the day Sylvie had been found bleeding to death, or so it had seemed. There was still some water in the tub, tinged red. My stomach churned.

"*Je suis désolé, mademoiselle,*" Renard said to me. "I'm sorry. I know this is upsetting to see."

Renard turned to Hobbs. "This is why I asked you to come. This..." He pointed to the water.

Hobbs smiled. "Tell me, Renard."

"I think I'm telling you what you already know, *oui?*" Renard was smiling, too. "We took a sample and found very little blood."

"Let me guess," Hobbs said. "Ox bile mixed with red paint pigment and some beet juice."

Renard laughed. "Hobbs, you are good. Very good."

―――

Renard took us to a café in Vernon for lunch that day. He laid out the criminal case as he saw it.

"I'm convinced the forgery was Legrand's idea," Renard said. "He had connections to make it happen. It probably wasn't the first time he had done this. A team in Paris is investigating other recent forgeries he may have been involved with."

"Do you think Sylvie was an accomplice?" Hobbs asked.

"It would seem she was complicit." Renard blinked rapidly, which I had noticed seemed to happen when he was excited.

"At what point?"

"Not at the beginning. Nothing suggests she knew Legrand before the day he visited Bonnard's house. All the sightings of them together were after that time."

"So when did he bring her to the dark side?"

"They were seen at a small hotel in Paris, the weekend of September 20 – two weeks after Sotheby's had authenticated the painting and about three weeks before the shipping crew arrived."

"Why is that significant?" Hobbs looked perplexed.

Renard leaned forward. "He made a big production of dinner. It wasn't her birthday or a special occasion. This was something more. He hired a concert violinist to play for her. A florist delivered a bouquet of roses that cost 100 euros. He personally arranged for amenities at the room. Cognac, chocolates, more flowers. The second night, he had a female massage therapist come to the room. She said he sat on the bed, drinking during the session, watching like a voyeur."

"Sounds a bit kinky. Bonnard-like, in fact." Hobbs was amused.

I smiled at Hobbs and Renard. "It sounds like a man desperately wooing a woman, after a bad argument maybe? Was he trying to win her back? Wanting to kiss and make up, in a big way?"

Renard blinked rapidly. "*Exactement*. My theory is that he proposed the forgery to her, after Sotheby's authenticated the painting. She reacted violently, rejecting the idea and him. Then he put on this big seduction."

"Do you think he loved her?" I asked Renard.

"*Pfff*, does it matter?"

"Yes, I think it matters a lot," I replied.

Hobbs looked at me. "Why do you say that?"

"If he loves her," I said, "he's probably planning a way, at this very moment, to spirit her away to his hiding place."

Hobbs grinned. "You'll be great on our TV show, Liz."

September 2014

SYLVIE

I REFUSED TO take Émile's calls. I was reeling from what he had proposed to me that night in my bed. I felt used and betrayed.

A few days later, I was online at the house and he called on skype. I let it ring a few times and then answered the call. I switched off my video, but I could see him.

"I can't see you," he said.

"I don't want to be seen by you."

"Sylvie, please, let me talk to you. I'm so sorry. Please believe me. I didn't mean to upset you."

"How did you think I would react?"

"I was stupid. Very stupid."

He asked me to meet him in Paris that weekend. I didn't say yes. But I didn't say no.

I quickly ended the call. But I had left the door open a crack and he kept his toehold.

He sent flowers to the house. He sent text messages of love and apology every day that week until I said yes.

He suggested we meet at an elegant boutique hotel on the Left Bank that Saturday evening. He had booked a table at the restaurant there — and as I later discovered, a room.

Dinner was sublime. He made every amend. A violinist serenaded us. A bouquet of roses arrived with dessert.

"I have a room for us here," he said quietly at the end of the meal. "Sylvie, I love you so much. I will never do or say anything that might hurt you again. Ever."

I acquiesced. I let him take me. He held his hand gently at my back as we walked up the hotel's spiral staircase. The room was filled with flowers. There was cognac and chocolates on the bedside table. From our little balcony, we had a view of the Eiffel Tower.

He slowly removed the layers of my armor. As he undressed me, he whispered, "Sylvie, please tell me you forgive me."

I forgave him that night, over and over. But I had a seed of doubt lodged in me, somewhere deep beyond his reach.

September 2015

LIZ

"Ox bile?" Kamal looked up from the eggs he was scrambling for me. "Where the hell do you get that?"

"It's a nutritional supplement – easy to get, usually in dried form though." I poured steamed milk into my coffee mug. "It also comes as a clear jelly and is used to suspend color pigments in water. I remember watching a paper marbler do this in Italy. Hobbs says it's a great ingredient for faking blood clots."

"But surely she knew they'd test a sample of the water, especially if her wrist cuts were superficial."

"I think she just went off the rails."

"How do you mean?"

"I'm wondering if she was supposed to get out of town soon after Legrand disappeared, before the forgery hit the headlines."

"They were going to run off together?"

"Yeah, that makes sense. She'd already paid him the commission, so they had funds to live comfortably, somewhere under the radar."

"Then why didn't she bolt?"

"I think she freaked out."

"Who found her in the tub?"

"Renard says she called a neighbor."

"So she wanted to be found."

I nodded. "Definitely."

"What's going to happen now?"

"She's basically under surveillance at her lawyer's estate. She can't go back to Giverny. Renard has locked her out of her own house."

"If they don't have grounds to arrest her, they're going to have to let her go home eventually."

"Eventually. But for now, I think they're waiting for Legrand to make a move."

"Has he tried to contact her?"

"I don't think so. But I bet he will."

"Why would he? He's got the money and the painting and no one knows where he is."

"He loves her."

Kamal smiled at me. "You're such a romantic."

Kamal and I were enjoying a nice balance in our relationship at that point. His four days in London each week allowed us both to focus on our work. Our long weekends together in Paris were all about us.

We loved our Left Bank neighborhood. We frequented the bistros, bookstores and quirky shops. My favorite was the

Autographes shop, an internationally renowned antique bookshop in the heart of Saint-Germain-des-Prés. The window display was full of rare editions and the writing samples of famous authors and artists: Marcel Proust, Francis Poulenc, Henry James, Auguste Rodin, Eugène Delacroix. Two letters, side by side, were written by Napoleon, who underscored his two-initial signature with a dramatic slash, and his wife Josephine, who favored flamboyant curlicues.

I began my forgery-detection training as an apprentice to a forensic document expert who tutored me on handwriting analysis. My specialty is signature authentication. I loved copying signatures as a kid and was good at aping my mother's handwriting if I needed a parent signature on a permission slip or a homework folder. I wasn't being devious. I was just a bit absentminded about the paperwork that came home in my school backpack.

My forensics mentor was very impressed when I once asked his opinion about the authenticity of two nearly identical documents, one of them a forgery. He studied them both for about 10 minutes and then correctly chose the original.

"But this copy is incredibly close," he said. "Who's the forger – do we know?"

"Yes." I smiled. "It's me." And then I showed him the forgery that had been submitted to us for evaluation.

"Yours is better than the forgery." He looked at me over the top of his reading glasses. "We need to keep your skills on this side of the law, Miss Jennings." He didn't take the matter lightly.

I had spent hours poring over Bonnard's signature. Later in his career, he signed his paintings simply as "Bonnard," with the stem of the "d" curving gracefully backward over the "r." The lettering had a calligraphic feel as line and curve went from thick to thin.

When the bogus *Renée* came back to Sotheby's in London, I looked at the painting's signature under magnification. To the unaided eye, it appeared authentic. But when magnified, the brush strokes told a different story. The clue was in the letter "o." The forger drew the "o" counterclockwise from the top. Bonnard drew it clockwise from the bottom.

September 2014

ÉMILE

I SPARED NO expense the weekend we spent holed up at the hotel in Paris. I needed to win Sylvie back to execute my plan. But I also desperately needed her in my life. She had become a sexual opiate to me.

On the second night, a female massage therapist came to the room. I had lit the room with candles that smelled of orange blossoms. I sat back on the bed and watched Sylvie disrobe and climb up on the table. As the therapist oiled her back, I poured myself some cognac and for the next hour let myself indulge my fantasies.

When the masseuse left, Sylvie was face up on the table, the sheet at her waist and her glistening breasts exposed. She dreamily opened her eyes as I stood next to the table. I slowly pulled down the sheet, imagining her sensual beauty on a Bonnard canvas.

It was the beginning of a long, lustful night.

Early the next morning, as we still lay in bed, I spoke to Sylvie about what had happened between us, wanting to be sure she knew my apology was sincere. Of course, I was hoping to be able to broach the subject of the painting again. But only if she was open to it. To my surprise, she was.

She asked if I was sure the copy would be exact. I explained the methods that would be used. She asked specifically about the paint and whether it could be matched to what Bonnard had used nearly 100 years ago. I assured her that the team Paul worked with was highly proficient.

The team was already at work, though I didn't tell her that as we lay in bed that morning.

"Sylvie, we have a nearly foolproof opportunity here. We're giving the world a copy of a major work by Pierre Bonnard. This is a painting that no one knew even existed."

"But the agents from Sotheby's and the Orsay saw the original. The switch should have been made before then."

"That's true. But I didn't come up with this idea until I saw how much the painting meant to you that day." I kissed her. "We can keep it and someday enjoy it together. We'll need to be careful about that, at least for a while."

"What will you do with it?"

"I have a couple of ideas. I know of safe places."

"We will be able to stay here, in France?"

"Most likely. It depends on how the auction goes. I'm hoping a private collector buys it. There's less likely to be scrutiny than if it goes to a museum."

She was quiet for a moment.

"What are you thinking, *chérie?*" I asked her.

She didn't answer.

"Sylvie, I love you." I stroked her cheek. "More than anything right now, I want you to believe that our happiness together is all I care about."

October 2014

SYLVIE

He was an hour late the night of the Lamberts' party. My thoughts went wild.

I had been uneasy ever since Émile put his plan in motion. I felt so exposed. My fingerprints would be all over this illicit plot if the forgery were ever discovered.

Émile assured me over and over that no detail had been overlooked. Every trace and trail would be concealed. I was certain he had done this before. I was in bed with a criminal with a successful track record, it would seem.

I had come to understand the stranglehold of erotic love and why Bonnard had kept two mistresses, sometimes under the same roof. He had a double addiction and couldn't wean himself from one to fully enjoy the other. I comforted myself with the thought that at least I wasn't competing with another woman for Émile's attention – none that I knew of. I couldn't bear to entertain that thought.

When I heard Émile at the gate that night at the party, I slipped out into the darkness and hurried toward him.

"I was so worried," I whispered.

"It's done." That's all he said.

I tucked my arm in his as we went inside.

It was late by the time we got to my place that night. We'd had a lot to drink at the Lamberts. But as was our ritual, the cognac and glasses came upstairs with us. I lit the candle by the bed and turned to Renée, the impostor, on the far wall.

In the shadows, she looked the same as the old Renée. The frame was the same. Everything about her seemed the same.

But as Émile and I made love that night, I felt there was a stranger in the room. As though Marthe had slipped behind a curtain, knowing my betrayal would be the undoing of me.

October 2015

KAMAL

I HAD GOTTEN an early train to Paris that Friday afternoon. I wanted to surprise Liz with champagne and hors d'oeuvres when she got home that evening.

There was a fantastic wine shop just down the street from her place that also carried French delicacies. I got some foie gras and escargot. My diet had certainly taken a sharp turn into the exotic unknown since I met Liz.

I stopped in at the corner shop, owned by our Kurdish friend Asan, whom I had gotten to know during my weeks with Liz in Paris. I appreciated Asan's view of Parisian culture. We were both foreigners here. His journey had been much more strenuous than mine, fleeing the Ba'ath regime of Saddam Hussein when he was a young man. He got off the plane in Paris and rode the Air France shuttle bus into the city. The terminus was the Air France corporate office.

As he told me that story one day, he shook his head. "I went into the Air France office and requested political asylum. Can you imagine that? And you know what's even more incredible? They said they would try to help me."

Asan and his wife, a lovely French woman, lived above the shop. His teenage nephew Tomar lived with them. Tomar was a quiet kid. I never sensed trouble with him.

Until that Friday, when I came in with the champagne and foie gras. I needed a few other things I knew Asan carried. When I walked in the door, no one was at the register, which I thought was strange. I could hear Asan shouting in the backroom. That was also a surprise. Asan was usually a mild-mannered guy.

He came through the beaded curtain that separated the shop from the backroom. Tomar followed him.

"Now do as I say, Tomar. I need you to unpack these boxes and get these things on the shelves. I've waited for you all day."

Asan's hands were trembling as he rang up my purchases.

"Are you okay?" I asked him quietly.

"No, Kamal, I am not." He looked at me wearily. "I am too old to be both an uncle and a father. The second job is much harder than the first."

I nodded. "Remember yourself as a teenager. Maybe that will help."

Asan shook his head. "I was nothing like him." He lowered his voice. "His friends are the problem."

I had seen Tomar a few times in a crowd of teen boys who hung out near the Metro station. Once I saw him kissing a pretty girl on a bench in a little courtyard near Liz's apartment. He seemed like a normal teen to me.

As I walked to Liz's place, I suddenly missed Yamir. It had been six weeks since I had left him with Aja in Mumbai. I skyped with him twice a week now. He loved those calls as much as I did. He always had something new to show me or something he couldn't wait to tell me about. At some point, I would need to insist on visitation rights. But for now, this was all I could hope for.

I opened the door to Liz's building and focused on the evening ahead. I would prepare a delicious *aperitif* for her. This would be an evening of celebration. It was three months ago, to the day, that I snared her cart at the airport. I smiled, wondering if she knew that had been no accident.

October 2014

ÉMILE

I HAD SET the alarm on my phone to ring at 5 a.m., but I was awake long before.

I hadn't wanted to leave the painting switch until the night before Sotheby's shipping agents arrived. But the paint on the forged copy had been slow to dry. Paul's team had mixed the pigments with an additive that essentially would age the paint to make chemical tests inconclusive. But they hadn't expected the drying time to be so long.

I was nervous about doing the transfer that morning. I had never been actively involved in physically handing over an original masterwork to the netherworld couriers who would make it disappear. I had been involved with the front-end operation – locating the work and arranging for others to do the handoff. But this put my actual fingerprints on the operation.

I wore gloves, as I carried the original *Renée* to my car, parked behind Sylvie's house. The painting was wrapped in layers of bubbled plastic and covered by a protective padded sheath.

Sylvie watched from the upstairs window. I stole one last look at her before getting in the car.

As I drove away, I had mixed feelings, of both elation and dread. Elation, if it all went well. Dread, if we had to set in motion Plan B.

I drove in the pre-dawn darkness to Paris, where Paul was waiting for me at a warehouse near Charles de Gaulle Airport. I didn't go inside. At this point, the less I knew, the better.

I opened the trunk.

"I'll let you know when it arrives," Paul said, as he removed the painting.

I nodded. That was all. The deed was done.

Afterward, I sat in my car, staring out the windshield at nothing, knowing I had indisputably crossed the line this time.

I called Sylvie when I got back to my apartment.

"The packers are crating the painting," she reported. "The Sotheby's agent just arrived."

I quietly thanked the cosmos for whatever had delayed the agent. *Renée, the Impostor*, as Sylvie called her, would be on her way to London by day's end. The first hurdle had been surmounted.

October 2015

LIZ

WHEN I GOT home from work that Friday evening, Kamal had champagne on ice. Edith Piaf was singing from the sound dock. Candles were lit, flickering in the twilight descending from the skylight.

"What's the occasion?" I asked him.

"A clash at an airport terminal, three months ago today, brought on by the forces of destiny." He took me in his arms and kissed me.

We drank and indulged in foie gras and escargot. Then he led me to my bed, where we made love under the ceiling's starry canopy.

Later, I lay there, catching my breath, gazing at the moon and stars. It was one of those perfect moments you want to remember for the rest of your life.

Kamal held me close. "I know it's too soon to ask this…"

"What?"

"Will you marry me?"

KAMAL

LIZ AND I walked around Paris the next day like newlyweds.

She had said YES.

We were going to be married. I didn't know when. But someday, in the not too distant future I hoped, we would be husband and wife.

I knew my divorce proceedings would drag on for another six months at least. But I wasn't contesting any of Aja's demands at that point. I was giving her everything she wanted — property, a stake in my financial holdings — hoping against hope she would allow me visitation privileges with Yamir.

But all I cared about that day in Paris was the woman who had said YES to starting a new life with me.

I bought Liz flowers. She posed with them on the steps of Notre Dame, pretending her lacy scarf was her bridal veil.

We shopped for an engagement ring at a jeweler I knew at Place Vendôme.

I took her to dinner that night to one of the finest restaurants in Paris. After dessert, the waiter brought me a little package on a silver tray.

The jeweler had done quick work. The ring fit perfectly.

I asked one more time, just to be sure. "Liz, my darling, will you marry me?"

She smiled at me, fingering the sparkling band of diamonds. "Yes, Kamal, yes."

October 2014

SYLVIE

My relationship with Émile wobbled after both paintings left my life.

I didn't miss The Impostor. Her one-night stand had left me feeling spied upon. I was happy to see her go.

But the empty space on my bedroom wall, where Bonnard's Renée had hung for years, left me feeling bereft. I had lost someone I cared about. In an odd way, I had always felt protective of that young girl on the bed. She had surrendered her virginity to a man old enough to be her father. Her flushed face, the gleam of sweat — or was it his saliva? — on her breasts, the telling smear of blood on the sheet. He had given her pain and pleasure she had never known. You could see that in her eyes. You could feel her breathlessness. Her hand lingered where he had been, where he had opened her wide. Had he told her to stroke herself, as he painted her? She was in his thrall. That was clear.

During my time with the Lamberts, when they weren't at home, I used to sit in that room, imaging Renée on the bed and the spectral figure of Marthe in the corner. What kind of man would enact this depraved fantasy in real life, apparently enjoying the torture he was inflicting on the two women he supposedly loved.

The toxicity of erotic love masked itself well, I had come to realize. You feel only the aphrodisiac thrill of lust and passion, the hormonal high of near-asphyxiating orgasms. But you don't feel, at first, the poison being released in your system.

―ᵒ―

Émile returned to Giverny that night, after the packing agents had taken away *Renée, The Impostor*. It had been quite a day.

We lay in bed at the scene of the crime, both feeling a bit shell-shocked in the aftermath.

"Will we recover from this?" I asked him in the darkness that night. The bedside candle had burned itself out.

He pulled me close to him and kissed me. "Sylvie, of course, we will. We have each other. That's what matters."

"We could have had each other without all this insanity." My voice sounded hard.

"Sylvie, are you sorry we did this?" he asked.

I could feel his breath on my face. I wanted to scream, *You did this! This was your idea, your doing.* But I was culpable, too. I had to own that now.

"Yes, I'm very sorry," I whispered.

"No, Sylvie, don't say that. There is no real crime in this. We shared something beautiful with the world and kept back a piece of it for ourselves."

I couldn't believe what I was hearing — a criminal rationalizing his crime. He rolled on top of me, rubbing against me. I spread myself open to him, as I had so many times before. But now, I could feel the toxin in my veins.

October 2015

KAMAL

A FEW DAYS after I asked Liz to marry me, I was back in London when a call came from Mumbai in the wee hours. I was stunned to hear my father's voice.

There had been a horrible accident. Aja's brother, Seth, had taken Yamir to nursery school that morning. They had been hit broadside by a bus. Seth was dead. Yamir was in intensive care.

"You need to get yourself on the next plane and come take care of your family." He voice cracked when he said *family*. But otherwise I heard no hint of emotion. He was ordering me, the despicable son, to come home.

"How bad is Yamir?"

"He's unconscious. There's internal bleeding. He was in the back seat of the car, on the side where the bus hit. He's lucky to be alive." He was quiet for a moment. "We are cremating Seth tonight."

I hated my father in that moment, for his dispassionate detachment. It was as if he were simply reporting the facts, the way some news anchors do as they read the teleprompter with no feeling for the tragedy they're reporting. Was he in shock? Sure. But did he hate me, too? Definitely, yes.

I told him I'd call him back when I had booked a flight. I clicked off the phone. I sat on the side of my bed and wept.

I went online and grabbed the first available flight that morning. And then I called Liz.

I cried, as she tried to comfort me. "My love, what can I do?" she asked. I could hear the panic in her voice.

"Nothing. I'll call you when I know more." I felt myself being sucked away from her, again. "Liz, I love you."

"I love you, too, Kamal. Call me when you get to Mumbai."

I stayed at the hospital that night, sitting at the bed of my critically injured son.

His chances were slim. I didn't need to hear that from the doctors. He looked like a bandage-wrapped mummy, with tubes coming out of his nose and mouth. His internal injuries were massive.

I leaned close and spoke to him, hoping he'd hear me somewhere in the ether he was floating in.

"Yamir, it's Daddy. I'm here." I held his little hand in mine. "I love you, Yamir. Please open your eyes."

LIZ

I waited for the phone to ring all day. I was constantly checking my messages, to see if there was news from Kamal.

He finally called late that night from Yamir's hospital room. Kamal had been crying, I could tell. "Liz, it's bad. Really bad."

"How bad?"

"They don't think he's going to make it."

"Oh, Kamal."

"He's barely hanging on. He's such a little fighter, though. I know he's trying. I keep telling him I'm here."

"Keep talking to him, Kamal. He can hear you."

"I hope so. " Kamal let out a sob. "God, I hope so."

We lived a nightmare in those days after the accident. I jumped every time my phone blipped with a message. Our conversations happened late during Kamal's night. He was camping out at the hospital, sleeping on a cot in Yamir's room.

Yamir had briefly opened his eyes, the day after Kamal arrived.

"He looked at me, Liz. He knew me. I'm sure of it." Kamal had been ecstatic.

But two days later, Yamir slipped into a coma. And three days after that, he died.

KAMAL

I WILL NEVER be able to think of Yamir in his last moments, without hearing the wailing of his mother. A woman who had, in the span of two months, lost her father, her brother and now, her only child.

From somewhere deep inside me, I felt a love for Aja that I didn't know I had. She lay next to her boy in his hospital bed, sobbing as she kissed his angelic face that peered out from the wrapping of his bandages.

I sat on the opposite side, kissing his hand. I thought I felt his fingers move. I wanted to believe they did.

And in the next instant, he was gone. I closed my eyes, imagining the flutter of his wings. Regretting everything I had done that may have contributed to his death, at the very tender age of four.

Could I have stopped this from happening, I kept asking myself. If I had been a better husband and stayed with my family in Mumbai, would I have been the one driving him to school that morning when the family driver called to say he was sick? Would we have left five minutes earlier or later that morning?

Would I have swerved in time to miss the bus? Would Yamir be alive if I had been driving that morning?

According to the Hindu tradition of cremation, a father may not light the funeral pyre of his deceased son. I couldn't have done it, even if it had been the custom. I had begged Aja to forget fucking tradition and bury him, as is usually done with young children. But she wouldn't hear of it. She wanted Yamir's spirit freed from his mangled bones.

As I watched the fire consume his little body, I felt like I was in a trance. I have no clear memory of this, but I'm told I walked toward the pyre, reaching for him, wanting to pull him from the flames. I was vaguely aware of cries of dismay when suddenly I felt a hard tug on my left arm. Someone was holding me back, yelling my name.

I turned around to see my father.

I stayed in Mumbai for another few days. I had dinner one evening with Aja and her mother and sisters. It was excruciatingly painful to be with them. Aja asked me to come to Yamir's room.

"Is there anything you would like?" she asked me. I was stunned and humbled by her kindness in that moment.

I looked at her and started to cry. "Aja…"

She reached out and touched my arm. "He loved you very much, Kamal."

On Yamir's bed was a little fuzzy bear that he adored. Aja handed it to me. "Take this, Kamal."

She turned away and left the room.

―⁌―

Before I left Mumbai, I called my father to ask if I could see him. He had agreed.

He was sitting in the salon when I arrived. He looked drawn. His cheeks were hollow, his eyes red from days of crying.

I stood until he asked me to sit.

He looked at me vacantly for a moment. "Would you have thrown yourself into the fire?" he asked.

I swallowed hard. "I may have. I wanted to hold him. Protect him." I gripped the arms of the chair. I couldn't let my father see me cry.

"You have been punished for your sins, my son. In ways you couldn't have seen when this all began." He stared out the window at a small bird sitting on the branch of a plumeria tree. "Yamir lives in your heart. You will feel him near sometimes."

We sat in silence for a few minutes. He shut his eyes. I could tell he badly needed sleep.

I rose quietly and went to him and kissed him on his forehead. He held onto my arm for a moment and squeezed it tight.

My mother appeared in the doorway, dabbing her tears with a hankie. I embraced her, feeling the warmth a child feels in his mother's arms.

I didn't know if I would ever see them again. But I would hold the memory of this moment, to light the dark days that I knew would come.

LIZ

I WENT TO Charles de Gaulle to meet Kamal. I couldn't let him face the arrivals hall with no one waiting for him.

I knew he was in big trouble the moment I saw him. He looked at me, as if in a daze, and said, "He was so beautiful. So beautiful."

Kamal and I planned to spend the weekend in Paris together. But on Monday, we would go to London, where I had already made an appointment with the therapist he had been seeing.

He slept a lot that weekend. We went out for short walks. Kamal always loved walking past the booksellers along the Left Bank, stopping to see what treasures lurked in the stalls.

I could see he had no interest in that. We walked as far as our favorite café. We sat outside, ordered our usual drinks. When we finished, he left money on the table and stood up to go.

It was like being with the ghost of Kamal's former self. This was far, far worse than the depression he fell into after he left Aja. He didn't tell me then about what had happened at Yamir's funeral. But that weekend, I didn't leave him alone for a second. I didn't trust him not to harm himself.

He sometimes looked at me like he wasn't sure what to say to me. He had no interest in intimacy. I reached for him in bed that first night and he turned away.

I lay in the darkness, looking up at that unblinking skylight. There were no stars that night. Just smoky clouds, reflecting the lights of the city.

I slipped my hand under my pajama top. I would have to keep my secret a while longer.

I was eight weeks pregnant.

March 2015

ÉMILE

I HAD HOPED Sylvie would come with me to London for the auction, but she was too anxious about the outcome and decided to stay in Giverny. I promised I would call her at the final gavel.

The excitement was palpable at Sotheby's that night. *Renée* sat on the stage of the main hall. It would be the final lot of the night. I knew the Orsay was going to be a serious bidder. But there was a rumor floating that a private collector in Hong Kong would enter the fray.

The Orsay's agent led the bidding at $1 million. The action escalated quickly. A Sotheby's agent on the phone at the front table reacted swiftly to every nod from the Orsay. There was a gasp in the room when the bidding topped $20 million. No one seemed to breathe as the Hong Kong bidder went to $30 million. The auctioneer held a fermata over that fever-pitch high note. Then the Orsay agent shook his head. I could see his disappointment. I knew how much the museum wanted it. But I was secretly glad *Renée, the Impostor* would be far from home.

The applause at the finish was explosive. I could barely get down the aisle, as colleagues — some delighted, others greenly envious — congratulated me.

I rushed out into the foyer and rang Sylvie. "You won't believe it, *chérie*. Thirty million!" She didn't respond at first. "Sylvie, did you hear me?"

"Yes, yes. My god."

"We have much to celebrate, my love. I'll see you tomorrow. I've booked our room."

I clicked off as Paul came up and embraced me. "We deserve a drink," he said.

I didn't get on the train back to Paris that night until late, feeling a bit sloshed and deliriously euphoric.

SYLVIE

On my train ride to Paris the next day, I felt happier than I'd been in a long time.

Renée's evil twin would be sent off to Hong Kong soon. I wouldn't have to see her at the Orsay, taunting me, threatening to reveal her secret. There would have been so many scrutinizing eyes on her there. But in her new home, she would be an exotic creature in a distant land, prized by her new owner and admired by a select few allowed to see her.

When I arrived at the hotel, the desk manager was expecting me.

"Monsieur Legrand is waiting for you in the room," he said, handing me a fob for the elevator keypad. "The penthouse, Madame."

I thanked him, unable to conceal my delight.

Émile opened the door, wearing only a robe. I playfully raised an eyebrow, which made him laugh.

"Oh, Émile." As he hugged me, I felt a release of tension I had been carrying for months.

"It's all behind us now." He kissed me. "Would you like to get into something more comfortable?"

My robe was laid across the bed.

He unzipped my dress. "Let me pour you some champagne."

October 2015

KAMAL

THE SESSIONS WITH my therapist saved me, but the road back from the brink was pure hell. I wanted to die. That's the simple truth. I had convinced myself that I had no reason to live. And even worse, I had no reason to believe that I deserved to live.

Liz went with me for the first few sessions after I got back from Mumbai. I could see the toll they were taking on her. How demoralizing it must have been for her to hear me say I had no reason to go on. I actually said that, with her sitting next to me, in the therapist's office one day. She burst into tears. How could she not.

The therapist suggested he see us individually for a while. That eased the strain at home. We had mutual counsel, insightfully guiding us through my recovery. He prescribed an anti-depressant, which helped me. I went to the gym. I got back to work. Liz was wonderful, so loving and patient.

One day, she was standing by the bedroom window, in a beam of sunlight that shone through her gauzy nightgown. She was twisting her lovely curly hair into a bun. As she lifted her arms, I could see the outline of her breasts and her belly. Her figure looked fuller.

I went to her and stood behind her, wrapping my arms around her. I stroked her tummy. "Is there something you want to tell me?"

She nodded.

"Is it what I think?"

"Yes," she said softly.

"How long have you known?"

"A while." She gently held my hand on her swollen belly. "I found out when you were in Mumbai."

"All this time you knew?" I turned her toward me. "And you didn't tell me?"

"Shhh." She put a finger to my lips. "I wanted to surprise you, when you felt better. When we could be happy about this."

"Are you happy?" I asked her.

"Very." She started to cry. "What about you?"

"My darling." I held her close. "Happier than I know how to say."

LIZ

Kamal couldn't stop talking about the baby. What names did I like, he kept asking. He went online and printed up boy and girl names, in English and Hindi.

"What about...?" he'd say over breakfast or on our walks around his neighborhood in Chelsea. The list of favorites grew. If it was a girl: Charlotte for my mother, Gaya for his mother, and Hadley and Leah just because we liked those. Boys, the same: Jared for my father, Rajiv for his father, and Daniel and Christopher. I was amazed he would consider naming a son after his father, given all the bad blood that had passed between them. The therapist said it was a very good sign.

It felt wonderful sharing every moment of this with Kamal. He went with me to the doctor, in London, for my first appointment. He asked her scads of questions: What vitamins did I need to take? What foods should I avoid? Should we not have sex?

He held my hand as the nurse moved a Doppler wand over my abdomen, searching for a heartbeat. As the seconds ticked away, I could see the worry on his face.

And then there was a *swoosh*. And another *swoosh* and another.

I smiled at Kamal as he squeezed my hand. He leaned down and kissed me.

"How I love you," he said.

May 2015

ÉMILE

Sylvie and I had talked about Plan B, if suddenly our scheme went sideways. But I never expected we'd have to implement it.

In the weeks after the auction, our lives returned to normal. Our new normal, as a newly rich couple. Sylvie gave me a 20 percent commission, which I tucked away in a Swiss account. I regarded this as our nest egg, our emergency fund.

She spent a lot of time with her tax accountant and an investment broker figuring out what do with the auction proceeds. She wanted to keep the house in Giverny, which suited me fine. I loved that part of Normandy and enjoyed my visits there. We had my Paris apartment in Montmartre. In essence, we had the best of both worlds.

Mostly, we wanted to travel for a bit. Sylvie told the Lamberts she would stay on until early summer. They had a big party coming up in May and needed her help. I had my usual work, helping museums locate paintings in private collections for exhibitions.

Paul called me one morning. I was still at the apartment. He said it was urgent. He'd meet me at a café on Place du

Tertre. I got there ahead of him and was reading the paper when I looked up and saw him rushing toward the table.

"There's trouble," he said, before he'd even sat down.

"What do you mean?"

"The Chinese are doing some tests on the painting."

"Who told you?"

"I have my sources." He pulled an envelope out of his jacket and laid it on the table. "You need to go."

"When?"

"There's a flight tonight." Paul patted the envelope. "Everything you need is here."

"Tonight? This is crazy."

"No, it's not. You need to go. We talked about this. Don't argue with me."

"What about Sylvie?"

"I will tell her. Just as we discussed. We have a plan, remember?" Paul looked at his watch. "You need to get packed. A driver will come for you at four."

"What if this blows over?"

"Then you'll come back in a couple of weeks and tell us all about your holiday."

"Is that what you think? That I'll be back in two weeks?"

"I hope so. For all our sakes."

"If not, when will Sylvie come?"

"I'm working on that now." Paul stood up. "You must go."

We embraced. "I'm worried about you, too."

"I'll be okay." He looked at me sternly. "There must be no communication between you and Sylvie. *None*."

I picked up the envelope from the table and tucked it inside my jacket. "By the way, where am I going?"

He lit a cigarette and inhaled. Then with a puff of smoke, he smiled and said, "Somewhere tropical."

When I got back to my apartment, I could think only of Sylvie. She and I had discussed what would happen if I had to *disappear*. But I had never really imagined this day. Paul would call her after I was on the plane that night. He would be our liaison from now on, until we could be reunited.

I quickly packed a bag. *Somewhere tropical.* No need for a suit and tie. After the sale, Paul had given me a checklist for this day, just in case. I focused on the essentials.

I also packed a few photos. I rolled up a sun hat Sylvie had forgotten on her last visit to Paris and stuffed it in the bag. She'll need it in the tropics, I told myself. But more than anything, I needed something tangible of her to hold on to. All other evidence of her – her toothbrush and hotel robe, a bottle of nail polish – I threw in a trash bag that I would drop at the dumpster on the way out.

I knew the police would empty every file and drawer. There was no paper trail linking Sylvie or me to the forgery.

I looked around my apartment. When would I see this place again, I wondered. Was I leaving behind my Paris life forever? Suddenly, the enormity of what I had done felt like a crushing weight.

SYLVIE

It was late when Paul called. I was just toweling off after my bedtime bath when the phone rang.

I was too stunned to speak at first. *Émile was gone?*

"I am making arrangements for you to leave, too," Paul said.

"Paul, what has happened?"

"The Chinese are authenticating the painting. This is serious, Sylvie. You must prepare yourself."

"For what?"

"To leave, of course."

"Leave? When?"

"In two days. I think I'll have everything set in two days."

In all the conversations Émile and I had had about his Plan B, I had always pushed the reality of it from my mind. And in that moment, with Paul talking about my imminent exit, I couldn't comprehend it.

"Paul, I can't leave."

"What? That's what we all agreed would happen. Émile expects you to join him."

"I'm not sure I can do it."

"Sylvie, you're dealing with the shock of this, I know. But you must go. It's the only way. If you stay behind and are implicated, you could go to jail."

I sat on my bed, with a towel wrapped around me, my hair dripping.

"Sylvie?"

"Call me tomorrow, Paul. I can't think straight."

⁂

I didn't sleep a wink that night. I lay staring at the bare spot on the wall where Renée and her impostor had hung.

I asked myself one question over and over: *Why had I allowed this to happen?*

Émile was gone. That changed everything. I would never see him again. I *couldn't* see him again.

In an act of betrayal that would have been unthinkable to me on the nights when he shared my bed, I made a decision that night: I would tell authorities he had duped and seduced me.

⁂

When Paul called the next day, I told him I couldn't leave.

He was livid. "You are being so stupid," he shouted. "Do you realize how much danger you are in?"

"I'm sorry, Paul. I don't have the nerves for this. The lying and sneaking around. I must face this as best I can."

"What will you tell the police?"

I knew Paul was worried that I might come clean.

"I will deal with the police when they come. If they come."

"It's not a question of *if*, Sylvie." Paul was nearly hissing at me. "It's a question of when. What do you want me to tell Émile?"

"That I loved him. I really did."

And then I switched off my phone.

November 2015

LIZ

My work on the Bonnard case essentially was finished. Hobbs was still up to his eyeballs though. Legrand remained at large, and his police file was growing fatter with evidence that he may have been an accomplice in other forgery cases. I had declined Hobbs' offer to get involved. I wanted a stress-free pregnancy. Our art-cop TV show would have to go on hiatus.

Kamal and I had decided to make our home in London. With a baby on the way, it seemed impractical to keep up our routine of spending weekends in Paris.

We had decided to spend one last weekend at my apartment, packing up my things and visiting our old haunts.

I stopped in to see Asan at the corner shop, to say good-bye. I could tell immediately something wasn't right. Boxes were piled up in the aisles. Asan was unshaven and bleary-eyed.

"What's wrong, Asan?"

He shook his head and said quietly, "Tomar has gone missing."

"What?"

"We have not heard from him in a month."

"Have you told the police?"

"There's nothing they can do. He is of adult age. He may do what he pleases."

"Where do you think he has gone?"

"I do not know. Perhaps he is living with friends here. We have not had an easy time with him in the past year."

"Maybe it's his way of separating. Being independent, striking out on his own." I looked at him with great empathy, thinking of the day when the child I was carrying would cross the bridge to adulthood. "But how painful this must be for you."

Asan wiped tears from under his glasses. "It is breaking my heart."

June 2015

SYLVIE

When the news broke of the forgery claim, I was in Giverny. I had just left work at the Lamberts and heard the report on the car radio.

It was a warm day. I wanted to stop at the Hôtel Baudy for a cool drink in the shade of the terrace. But I went straight home. I parked in the back as usual. I went inside the house and quickly drew the curtains and bolted the doors. I really thought for a day or two I could hide from this.

The media attention didn't come to me immediately. That surprised me. But a police detective was at my door the next morning. His name was Inspector Renard. He gave me his card and said he had a few questions for me.

I invited him inside. We sat together in the living room.

He wanted to know how I had come to own the Bonnard painting and if it had ever been appraised or exhibited. I assured him it had been hidden from view since Bonnard gave it to my grandfather after Renée's suicide in 1925. He asked why I had decided to sell it.

"I always had planned to sell it someday — it was my retirement savings," I told him. "Monsieur Legrand had good connections and said he could help me. He arranged for Sotheby's to see it. Two curators from the Orsay were here that day, too. They all seemed sure it was genuine. In fact, they thought it was *significant* — that's how they described it. I can't understand why the Chinese think it's a fake."

"I haven't seen the forensic reports yet," he said. "More testing will be done, but that will take some time. You have the opinions of respected experts on your side. But there's an allegation of fraud and it is our job to conduct an investigation." Renard seemed almost apologetic, which gave me some comfort.

He looked around the room. "Where did you display the painting?"

"In my bedroom."

"When did you meet Monsieur Legrand?"

"Last year. He came to see the Bonnard house in Vernonnet. I work for the owners."

"How would you describe your relationship with him?"

"We had similar interests and enjoyed each other's company."

"Was it more than that?" His eyes held mine.

I took a breath, trying to steady myself. "Yes, we were romantically involved."

"You said *were*. Are you still seeing Monsieur Legrand?"

"Actually, I haven't seen him in a few weeks."

"Has there been a problem between you?"

"We've both been quite busy lately."

"Do you believe he's in Paris?"

"I don't know. He travels some."

"How much did you pay him for his services?"

I sensed he was trying to probe a tender spot with me, but I kept myself in check. "Six million dollars."

"Madam Chastain, do you have any reason to believe he has left the country?"

"As I told you, Inspector, I don't know where he is."

That wasn't a lie.

―⸺―

The next day, Paul called me from a pay phone, which was his habit. I told him about Renard's visit.

"Do you have any idea how bad this is going to be for you?" he asked. "Émile is beside himself with worry."

"About what exactly?"

"About *you*. God, Sylvie, he loves you. Have you conveniently forgotten that?"

I had begun to demonize Émile in my revisionist version of our story. It was jarring to hear Paul speak of love.

"I'll be fine."

I wasn't sure of that, not with the growing attention the case was getting. But there was no way I could go to Émile and live the life we had fantasized about. That dream was over.

ÉMILE

I HAD DISAPPEARED into a surreal world. Paradise was at the doorstep of my bungalow, nestled in a grove of banana palms. Every morning, I walked a pristine white beach and imagined the day when Sylvie would join me in this new life we had envisioned.

I had wi-fi and read the news daily of what was happening with the forgery case. I was baffled when reports began surfacing of Sylvie's story.

Over and over she said: *I knew nothing.* She claimed I had seduced her to gain access to the painting. After she paid me the commission, I disappeared with the money, leaving her with an empty promise that we would grow old together.

Paul was more than baffled. He was outraged. "She doesn't love you, Émile. Forget her. Do you hear me? You've got a tidy sum to live on. But don't think for a second about sharing any of it with her."

He and I talked about the original *Renée*, which had safely arrived at its destination in Switzerland. In a few years, we could pass it through *channels*, as we referred to the labyrinthine pathways paintings sometimes traveled, to an attic cachet of forgotten artwork that had been bequeathed by a private collector to his ignorant nephew. Paul and I were good at fabricating such stories.

But the story of Sylvie and me would take me a long time to erase. I truly loved her and hoped she would come to her senses. I knew if I could see her again, everything would be fine.

November 2015

KAMAL

My dark days slipped away when I knew I was going to be a father again. I felt guilty about feeling happiness so soon. I had just lost a child and was preparing to bring another into the world. My therapist and I discussed this at length, about how to balance my grief with my joy.

Liz and I had come back to Paris, for one last stay at her place. She didn't have much to pack up. We would make quick work of it, then enjoy our time here together. The last days of our honeymoon, in a way. When my divorce was final, we would marry and go away for another honeymoon. Maybe to Provence, where all of this began.

We arrived in Paris on a Wednesday. Liz had gone down to Asan's shop to get a few things. I knew she would miss this neighborhood and her Parisian life. But we had so much to look forward to in our new life together in London.

I sat on Liz's bed and looked at the Bonnards on the walls. The nudes of Marthe. The one of Renée, with the spot of blood between her legs, which I wouldn't have noticed if Liz hadn't shown it to me.

There seemed to be a monster within this man, Bonnard. One of his Marthe nudes called *Woman Dozing on a Bed* appears to show a bestial figure in the foreground, blowing smoke toward her vagina. Another similar shape seems to be etched in the bedsheets, its mouth open wide as though it's about to devour her.

I wondered what kind of a lover Bonnard was. He seemed nerdish in his photos. Hardly the image of a man who could make women succumb to him.

I started removing the prints from the walls. I wouldn't miss these images. I wanted nothing but a world of happiness with Liz. I had been given an extraordinary gift of a second chance at love, which until I met her, I had never known.

September 2015

SYLVIE

I COULD FEEL myself coming undone. Every day, there were reporters at my door. Photographers followed me around the village. The story had become a soap opera played out by the media.

Paul kept his communication with me to a minimum. My brief conversations with him were always tense. On our last call, I hung up on him after he shouted at me: *What the hell are you doing?*

I had no clue what I was doing at that point.

The forensic team hired by Sotheby's had determined the painting was a forgery, based on a test of paint samples. I knew the authorities suspected me as an accomplice. Each morning I awoke fearing that the police would be at my door with a warrant for my arrest.

I had to convince them I was an innocent woman who had fallen in love with a thief.

One night, when I was soaking in the tub, the thought of suicide came to me. I imagined how I would do it. How I could *fake* it, to make it appear that I had tried to kill myself. Wouldn't my accusers believe me then? The spurned lover who had plunged into the depths of despair – so like the lovelorn Renée who had taken her own life when Bonnard cast her aside.

I planned it carefully. I read about how to cut myself to produce enough blood without making a fatal slice. I made some fake blood, too, to make it all seem real.

I slipped into the tub that night, with a steak knife resting on the soap dish and my phone within reach.

As blood trickled down my arm, I pretended I was purging poison from my veins. I called my neighbor, telling her I felt violently ill. Would she call an ambulance for me, I asked. And then I dropped the phone to the floor.

ÉMILE

When I heard the news of Sylvie's attempted suicide, my new world in paradise imploded.

Paul told me of his last conversation with her and how she seemed so irrational.

"She was extremely stressed by all the attention," he said. "The press was at her door. The police had questioned her several times. She was sure she was going to be arrested."

"What will happen now?"

"I've heard there's an attorney who's advising her. He likes cases that get a lot of publicity."

"There's no hope of her leaving now."

"None, Émile. Forget about her. I tell you, she's nothing but trouble now."

I learned to appreciate the artistry of forgery early in my career. In my mid-20s, I went to work for my uncle who was an art dealer in Paris. He had a degree in art history from the Sorbonne. At his insistence, I, too, had studied art history at the Sorbonne.

His art-history background made him an astute connoisseur. He claimed that at least a third of all artworks passing through high-end channels were counterfeit. "If you want to deal in fine art," he used to tell me, "you need to think like a con artist."

Too often art dealers and auction houses are complicit in the forgery trade, turning a blind eye to suspicious claims of provenance in their greed to collect hefty commissions.

My uncle prided himself in being able to recognize fakes. He had a good track record and was often called upon to provide an expert opinion in forgery cases. Nowadays, technology delivers the verdict. But in his time, he relied on gut instinct and his academic knowledge of great artists' tools and techniques. He loved unveiling pretenders, some of them quite accomplished.

During the summer of 1989, when I was 25, my uncle sent me to Florence to meet a friend of his by the name of Paolo Bartolucci who worked as a conservator at the Uffizi Gallery. It was no coincidence that Paolo had a lovely daughter who was my age and unmarried. Her name was Milana. I happily allowed myself to be caught up in my uncle and Paolo's conspiratorial matchmaking as I spent that summer under Paolo's tutelage.

Paolo taught me about the fundamentals of Renaissance painting. I learned about the weave of canvases, the composition and textures of paper, and how pigments were extracted from plants and stone. Paolo showed me how to recognize a brush's telltale markings in the paint and even the animals the bristles came from – boar, deer, squirrel or sable. Paolo often referred me to Italian painter Cennino Cennini's *Il Libro dell'Arte*, written in the early 1400s and essentially a Renaissance artist's how-to guide. Restoration artists today use it as their bible – and surely more than a few forgers have used it as a reference as well.

The fine line for me between the evil and good of forged art blurred soon after Milana and I began our affair that summer. Our interactions were quite chaste at first. I was a guest in their home and thought it better to err on the side of caution with Milana. I wasn't convinced she would welcome a bold overture from me, so I hung back, enjoying how she slowly warmed to me.

Milana was multi-lingual with a good command of French. My Italian was passable. But as Milana and I spent more time together, our common language was French. She worked part-time as a translator for a university press. She was well read and a marvelous conversationalist. There was something hypnotic about her when she spoke. The sparkle in her dark eyes and the musical inflection of her laugh captivated me, along with her classic Italian beauty.

The Bartoluccis' home sat on a hillside on the south bank of the Arno, where mercifully there was a bit of a breeze on stifling hot afternoons. Paolo and I would break up the work day by coming home for lunch, which typically was a four-course Tuscan feast – an antipasti platter, followed by pasta or risotto and then a meat dish, and, of course, a delectable dessert – prepared by his wife, Luisella. Paolo would often take a short nap afterward, before we would go back to the Gallery. But I'd roll up my sleeves and help Luisella and Milana clean up. Initially, they objected, but I insisted. I enjoyed their company and they, mine. I began to feel part of their family.

Some days during the quiet of afternoon *riposo*, Milana and I would sit in the shade of the garden. I was always mesmerized by the sweeping view of Florence's iconic landmarks. The cathedral with its enormous tiled dome and monumental *campanile* never failed to take my breath away. And as the summer days passed, Milana did the same.

It all started with a tender kiss in that garden one evening. It wasn't easy for us to manage more than that at first. Her parents were always nearby. But once we'd felt the spark of passion, it became increasingly difficult to keep the fire at bay.

One warm night, I couldn't sleep and went out to the garden to cool myself. Milana, too, had been restless and had seen me from her bedroom window upstairs. What happened next seemed like a dream as she walked through the garden in a white nightgown that glowed in the moonlight. We were both terrified of being caught, which made everything about our lovemaking that night more intense.

She was a virgin, which surprised me. When she stood up from our grassy bed under an olive tree by the terrace, I saw a spot of blood on her white nightgown.

I felt enormous guilt in the days that followed our night in the garden. I had deflowered an exquisite rose. But I knew I was falling in love with her, which I believed would make everything right in the end.

We kept a safe distance for a week or so. But it was excruciating for us both. Then one night, she came to me in my room, on the ground floor behind the kitchen in what once had been maids' quarters. She stood in the darkness with her back against the door, which she had closed quietly. I knew I should have sent her away. But, of course, that didn't happen.

I felt like I had slipped into a testosterone-induced haze as the weeks passed that summer. Paolo and his wife seemed pleased with our budding romance. Perhaps Paolo sensed there was more happening between us than an affectionate flirtation. But I'm sure Luisella, a good Catholic woman, would have been horrified if she knew Milana was often in my bed.

One weekend afternoon, Paolo and Luisella had gone into town on an errand. Milana and I were alone, finishing lunch on the terrace, when she asked nonchalantly, "Has my father told you about his art collection?"

It was news to me that Paolo was a collector. He had never mentioned it nor had any of the modest paintings in the main rooms of the house suggested anything extraordinary.

She took me by the hand. "Come."

I hadn't been on the upper floor of the house and felt like a trespasser as she led me down a sunlit corridor into her parents' bedroom. The windows were adorned with silks and brocades, her mother's touch. On the wall opposite the bed, there appeared to be a shuttered window. But I quickly realized it was on an interior wall.

"An illusion," Milana said softly, as if reading my mind.

She carefully opened the shutters and pulled the cord to a velvet curtain that masked a painting. A masterwork.

It was by 16th-century Florentine Mannerist Jacopo Pontormo. I had seen the same painting at the Uffizi. I stepped closer, looking for the clues that Paolo had trained me to see. But my common sense wasn't allowing me to believe the painting was an original.

I looked questioningly at Milana, waiting for an explanation.

She sighed and turned away from me, walking over to a window that framed the spectacular view of Florence.

"It's a complicated story," she began. "He has others, too."

"How did he get them?" I could barely ask the next question. "Are they stolen?"

"I think he considers them *on loan*."

We heard a car approaching on the road below the house.

Milana abruptly moved away from the window. "We must go." She pulled the curtain cord to cover the painting and closed the shutters.

It wasn't until later that night, when Milana came to my bed, that I heard the full story.

When Paolo was an apprentice at the Uffizi as a young art student, one of his mentors, Enrico Moretti, was under investigation for forgery. Many of the Gallery's masterpieces had been carted off by the Germans during World War II. But some had slipped surreptitiously into the hands of private Italian collectors who believed they were doing a great service to posterity by hiding these masterpieces in their homes and secret vaults. Moretti was among them. In the years after the war, amid the chaos of rebuilding Italy, documents were lost, memories were blighted. But in time, the dust cloud lifted. When Moretti sensed he was under suspicion, he had already pulled his young apprentice into the shadows.

"Papa hid the originals, to help protect Moretti, who felt he had done nothing wrong," Milana told me. "He had saved invaluable masterpieces from the hands of Nazi looters and believed he had acted heroically."

"But Moretti didn't give the paintings back to Italy."

"He pretended to, claiming they had been discovered in a wine cellar at an old Tuscan villa. Actually, they were copies he had commissioned – as beautiful as the originals – that he hung at the Uffizi."

I'll never forget that moment. Milana was curled up next to me, her head on my chest as I stroked her hair. I closed my eyes, realizing the implication of what she was saying. I had examined those paintings on the walls of the Uffizi, unknowingly with their master artist at my side.

"Was your father the forger?"

"Yes," she said quietly. "Yes."

Paul's words *forget about her* pounded in my head that day as I walked along the empty beach by my Tahitian hideaway. I thought of Milana and how I had let her go after her revelation about her father. She loved me and wanted me to know her family secret. I loved her, too, but I had scruples instilled by my uncle, who I was certain knew nothing of Paolo's crime. I couldn't and wouldn't let my knowledge of what he had done in any way taint my uncle's sterling reputation, so I cut myself loose.

I left Florence a week later. Paolo was sad to see me go and even sadder that Milana and I suddenly had turned away from each other. She was angry that I had ended our affair and worried that I would betray her father. I assured her I wouldn't and, about that, I kept my word. She tearfully defended him – he had been young and recklessly eager to flaunt his talent. Moretti had died of a massive heart attack on the day he was arrested, which was a blessing for Paolo, who kept the original masterpieces hidden away for years. But later in his life, he enjoyed them in privacy, convincing himself they were *on loan*, entrusted to him for safekeeping.

It would be some time before I, too, would cross the line. As I made an irreproachable reputation for myself in the museum world, privy to the holdings of private collectors, the door eventually opened to the art of deception. When I met Paul, my scruples slowly disappeared.

For years I'd had access to masterworks that were rarely seen and in some cases, previously unknown. I often thought of Paolo, and envied him, with a Pontormo behind a velvet curtain in his bedroom.

But more than anything, as I looked out at the sea that day, I wanted Sylvie in that bedroom. And in the mess I had created, I had lost her, too.

November 2015

LIZ

When I told Kamal that evening, as we lay in bed, that Tomar had gone missing, I started to cry. I knew my hormones were partly to blame, but I truly felt Asan's pain.

"Has Asan reported this to the police?" Kamal asked.

"It seems there's not much they can do. Tomar is 18 and free to do as he pleases. He left in the middle of the night. No explanation. No good-bye." My tears suddenly turned to sobs.

Kamal held me close. "Your maternal instincts are kicking in."

I felt a wave of anxiety crashing over me. "Kamal, do you think I'm going to be a good mother?"

"You're going to be a wonderful mother."

"How do you know?"

"Look at you," he said, wiping the tears from my face. "You weep for a boy – and the man who raised him – as though they were your own family. Your heart is full of love – for life, for me, for this child inside you." He rubbed my belly.

And in that instant, I felt something I had never felt before – our baby's first little kick. My heart was overflowing with love.

November 2015

SYLVIE

IT HAD BEEN two months since I had moved to my attorney's estate near Versailles. Émile was still missing. Paul had gone quiet. No charges had been brought against me. I was beginning to sleep better. I felt less anxious, more hopeful about the future.

I started thinking about making a fresh start. I could sell the house in Giverny and get a small apartment in Vernon or maybe somewhere else where I wouldn't be known. I'd find a job – I daydreamed about working in a bookstore or a flower shop. I longed for normalcy again.

But that wasn't to be. One morning, Laurent, my attorney, came to see me after breakfast. I usually took breakfast alone in my suite at the far end of the house, where I had some privacy. It was a comfortable space with a sitting room and kitchenette adjoining the bedroom, overlooking the walled back garden that, on that day, was tinged with autumn hues.

Laurent was dressed in a smartly cut suit. In his mid-40s, he was married to his career. No wife. No children. With his charm and good looks, he was a catch, which brought him a steady stream of female clients, some hoping for more than legal advice. There had been nothing untoward between us. He was extremely professional, always protective and kind. I knew he had taken the case for the publicity it would bring him. But I believed he genuinely cared about what might happen to me.

I got a whiff of his cologne as he sat down next to me on the overstuffed sofa. Gaultier. Émile's favorite.

"I don't have good news," he said grimly. "The police have interviewed your neighbor, who claims she saw Émile take what appeared to be a wrapped painting from your home early in the morning on the day Sotheby's packers were there."

I suddenly felt a knot form in my chest. Laurent's eyes were fixed on me, gaging my reaction. My mind raced through the versions of the story I had told. I never disputed that Émile and I went back to my place the night of the Lamberts' party. But over and over, I had sworn I knew nothing about what he had done.

"She said it was quite early, just before daybreak."

"If it was dark, how could she see what he was carrying?"

"Apparently, there's a street light that illuminates your back garden."

"I was asleep when he left," I said with certainty.

"Sylvie." Laurent cleared his throat. "Your neighbor says she saw you at the window watching him leave."

―⚬―

My hand shook as I tried to dial Paul's number on my mobile phone. No answer. I quickly sent him a text: *Urgent! Call me.*

I frantically looked around the bedroom and started stuffing clothes into my suitcase.

I hadn't meant to lash out at Laurent, but I had felt like a trapped animal.

"There's growing suspicion of you," he had said. "An arrest warrant may be next."

"On what grounds?"

"As an accomplice."

"I had nothing to do with the forgery!"

"But if you knew of a forgery – and apparently, you do – you are not innocent in this."

"So now you think I'm a criminal?" I had asked him accusingly.

"I think you haven't been telling me the whole truth."

I had heard the anger in his voice, which had made me more defiant. "I want to leave. I want to go home. Now."

"You're free to leave, Sylvie. You're not a prisoner here."

My mind was spinning. I had to call Paul. "I'll leave this morning."

"Where will you go?"

"Home. I'll go home."

"It's a quarantined crime scene. You can't go home."

It was then that I had burst into tears.

How had I let this happen? I had played my hand perfectly, or so I thought.

I pulled shoes from the closet along with a bag of laundry and threw everything into the suitcase.

Finally, my phone rang. It was a woman's voice I didn't recognize. She gave me the address of a bar in Versailles' city center and said, "I'll meet you there at noon."

⁂

I was a wreck when I came downstairs later that morning. Laurent helped me with my bag. He had called a taxi, which was waiting outside. I had told him I was going to meet a friend.

As I got in the cab, Laurent leaned toward me – the scent of Gaultier suddenly made me miss Émile – and handed me his card. He had written a number on the back. "This is my private line," he said. "Call if you need me. Anytime." He patted my arm.

Twenty minutes later, I stood in the entryway of a bar in central Versailles, wondering who might greet me. I had hoped Paul would be there. But instead, a young woman approached me. She was petite, in paint-splattered cargo pants and a T-shirt, with tinted wire-rimmed glasses and green streaks in her blond hair that was pulled back in a messy knot. She called herself Nanette.

"My car is parked in the back," she said, motioning for me to follow her.

I stood rooted in place. "Where's Paul?"

"Not to worry, Sylvie," she said quietly. "He is behind all of this.

I followed her as she took my suitcase and rolled it through the bar, down a hallway that led to a back door. When we stepped outside, into an alley, Nanette turned to me, with her hand out. "Give me your phone."

"Why?"

"Sylvie, please do as I ask. Give me your phone."

I reluctantly took it from my handbag and handed it to her.

To my horror, she slammed it against the building's brick wall and threw the shattered pieces into a nearby dumpster.

"What the hell?" I shouted at her.

She took me by the arm. "Sylvie, stay calm. You're not in danger. But we have to be cautious."

She quickly got me and my bag into her car, an old beat-up Citroën that smelled of varnish and paint.

As she started the engine, I wanted to run, but it was too late for that. "Where are you taking me?"

"My place. It's about 20 minutes from here." I knew she sensed my panic. "Sylvie, try to relax."

She drove through the backstreets until we were out of the city limits. I have a terrible sense of direction. I tried to piece together our route, but it was futile. Occasionally, I'd catch sight of a sign pointing to a place I'd heard of. But soon I gave up trying to figure out where we were.

En route, Nanette told me I was booked on a flight that night out of Paris.

"Where to?" I asked.

"I'll explain everything when we get to my place."

We passed through an industrial area, with abandoned warehouses, bordered by a block of rundown apartment buildings. She pulled into a dimly lit parking garage below one of them.

She apologized for the mess as we entered her dingy studio apartment. The room was spacious, but it was cluttered with painting supplies and canvases. I noticed a heat lamp in the corner of the room along with old paintings that had been partially scraped. I wondered if Nanette was part of Paul's forgery operation.

"We don't have much time," she said, handing me a small plastic bag.

"What's this?"

"Your new hair color."

"No."

"Sylvie, please don't argue with me. You're on a watch list. You must try to disguise yourself."

Nanette had once worked in a hair salon, so the outcome wasn't disastrous. Within an hour, I went from brunette to blond. And with a flurry of scissor snips, I had a stylish shag. I barely recognized myself.

She had a new wardrobe for me as well. I changed out of my tailored trousers and silk blouse. My traveling outfit was jeans and a loose-fitting T-shirt under a bulky sweater.

Nanette handed me a pair of sneakers to complete the makeover.

"I'll wear my own shoes," I said firmly.

Nanette looked at my leather flats, in the context of my new hip-casual attire, and shrugged. "It works."

Nanette made tea and we sat down on her tattered sofa. She dumped everything in my handbag on the coffee table. She removed my driver's license and credit cards from my wallet and, despite my protests, cut them into small pieces.

"You can keep the cosmetics," she said, as she pushed my lipstick and makeup toward me. She handed me a small shoulder bag. "Your new passport is inside."

Not only did I have a new look, but a new identity as well. My new name: Claudine Roussel.

The passport photo also captured my new blond self. "Impressive," I said to her.

"We forgers are good at this."

She gave me a pay-as-you-go phone. "It has more minutes than you'll need where you're going."

"Where am I going?"

"Somewhere tropical." She unzipped a carry-on bag sitting beside the sofa. "You won't need much. A few changes of clothes, a swimsuit, underwear." She held up a pair of flip-flops.

"What about these things?" I looked over at my own suitcase.

"They'll be safe here with me."

I doubted she thought I'd be coming back soon. The contents of my suitcase probably would meet the same demise as my phone.

A short while later, I was in a car with a male driver who took me to Charles de Gaulle Airport. We rode in silence until he pulled up at the Sheraton. He told me to go to the bar next to the lobby. "A man will ask you if you'd like a drink," he told me. "Listen carefully to what he has to say."

At the entrance, a hotel porter insisted I check my bag with him. I didn't argue. The fight had gone out of me.

I sat at the bar and within a few minutes, a man about my age joined me. "Would you like a drink?" he asked. "You seem a bit jittery."

"I'd love a drink."

"Cognac?"

I tried not to smile. Apparently, Émile was an accomplice in this scheme as well.

My bar buddy ordered the drink and then handed me a small package, the size of a business envelope and wrapped with a bow. "I know it's not your birthday, but it's a day worth celebrating." He leaned close to me and whispered, "Go into the ladies room after you've finished your drink and open it. It has everything you need." He kissed my cheek, then slid off the barstool. "Bon voyage."

I quickly drank the cognac and went to the ladies room. I locked myself in a stall and tore open the package. Inside was a travel wallet with a currency I didn't recognize, along with a ticket. I looked at the destination: TAHITI. Émile's handprints were everywhere in this.

I made my way to the airport's Schengen Passport Control checkpoint. The line was unusually long. Armed soldiers patrolled the area – the new normal in post-Charlie Hebdo Paris.

I finally got to the window and slipped my passport under the plexiglass barrier. The agent looked at the photo and then back at me. He summoned a short man with a thin, dark moustache who was in the next cubicle. I recognized him immediately as one of the detectives who had questioned me.

I waited as he scanned my passport and studied the computer monitor. Did he recognize me, I wondered. He asked to see my boarding pass.

"Where is your return ticket?" he asked, blinking rapidly.

I hadn't looked at the itinerary. I rummaged through my bag and produced the voucher for the e-ticket, which showed I would be returning in two weeks. I couldn't imagine that would actually happen.

He stamped my passport. "You must go through luggage inspection at security." He pointed to a metal table by the security check-in area.

There wasn't much to show the baggage screeners, who carefully removed everything in my suitcase: A few cotton dresses, a couple of T-shirts, a pair of shorts, a swimsuit, lacy underwear and flip-flops. I wondered if Émile had requested the lacy underwear.

An hour later, after a stiff drink at a bar by the boarding gate, I was on the plane. I closed my eyes as the last passengers settled in and the crew prepared for takeoff.

What I didn't see, but learned of later: In the minutes before the doors closed, Inspector Renard boarded the plane.

November 2015

LIZ

HOBBS WAS BACK in Paris the week Kamal and I were packing up my apartment. I had stopped by my office at the Orsay to pick up some things and saw him in the hallway.

"Am I happy to see you!" He grinned like a Cheshire cat. "Come with me."

I followed him to his office. "This came in last night." He made a few clicks on his computer screen and pointed to a grainy surveillance photo of a woman passing through security at Charles de Gaulle.

"Do we know her?"

"Take a closer look." Hobbs enlarged the image.

"Incredible! What a transformation." Sylvie looked a bit like Bonnard's gilded version of Renée. "So where's she going?"

"Tahiti."

"Into the arms of Émile?"

His eyes twinkled. "Let's hope so."

November 2015

SYLVIE

My connecting flight out of L.A. was delayed, which meant I didn't arrive in Tahiti until late afternoon the next day. A driver was waiting for me at the airport in Papeete. He held a card that read *C. Roussel*. It took a moment for that to register.

He told me we had a bit of a drive. I was beyond exhausted. I curled up in the back seat and fell asleep.

I awoke an hour later as the car bumped along an unpaved road. I sat up and looked out the window.

I had never been to Tahiti. I remembered the night when Émile and I, soaking in my tub, had talked about coming here together. I had been deeply in love with Émile then and couldn't imagine anything more wonderful than being here with him.

It had been six months since I'd seen Émile. We'd had no communication except through Paul, who surely had tried to convince him to give up on me. I had publically denounced Émile. I repeatedly had painted him as a liar and a thief. How could he possibly want me here with him now. In the tumult of the past few days, I hadn't allowed myself to think about the reality of stepping out of this car and being face-to-face with him again. Would he lash out at me in anger? Would he demand explanations? I had been too distracted by the suddenness of all of this to come up with a plan. At that moment, I was bone tired. I just wanted to sleep.

As I looked out at the lush tropical landscape, I could see the exotic, colorful motifs of a Gauguin painting. Although I was drawn to his work, I was repulsed by Gauguin the man — a syphilitic who sexually preyed on the young Tahitian girls he painted. Bonnard was almost a saint compared to Gauguin.

We turned down a narrow dirt road, shaded by trees choked with vines. It ended in a secluded clearing, where there was a bungalow partially obscured by banana palms. Beyond the clearing was a beautiful white-sand beach.

My legs felt weak as I stepped out of the car.

Émile appeared on the porch. He seemed a bit thinner. His hair was grayer. My heart raced, with dread or delight — I wasn't sure.

I stood by the car, as the driver took my bag inside. I knew he would gone in a few minutes, leaving me alone with Émile. For a second, I felt panicky. But as Émile walked toward me, I knew I had nothing to fear.

I was vaguely aware of the car leaving, as Émile held me close. "Sylvie, I thought this day would never come. I've been so worried about you." He rubbed my back and kissed my hair. Finally, he pulled away to take a good look at me. "I can't believe it's really you."

"The hair was not my idea."

He laughed. "I like you as a blonde."

He put his arm around me and took me inside.

"Welcome," he said. "It's modest, but comfortable – with a fantastic view." The living room-dining area had a wall of windows that looked out onto the beach.

The room seemed to tip a little or maybe it was just me. "Émile, I'm so tired."

"You must be, *chérie*. Come."

He led me down a hallway into a bedroom. I quickly slipped out of my clothes. He pulled aside the mosquito netting that hung from the bed's canopy as I crawled under the sheet. I lay back against the pillows and looked up at him. I could see tears in his eyes.

He quickly undressed and slid into bed next to me. He stroked my arm and looked at the faint scars on my wrists. "What were you thinking?"

"I had to make them believe me."

"It must have been awful for you."

"Please, let's not talk about it now."

"No, not now."

I let him make love to me. I had almost forgotten how wonderful he could make me feel. I let everything fall away as he brought me to a climax. I gave him pleasure, too. We were lovers again, pretending that something horrible hadn't happened between us. I will always remember that night as a gift.

I fell asleep in his arms to the soothing rhythm of the surf. The last words I heard him say, as I drifted off, were *Sylvie, I love you*.

⁂

I woke up early the next morning, before dawn. Émile was sound asleep. His face was a few inches from mine. I'll never forget how content he looked.

My heart ached as I slipped out of bed and quietly got dressed.

I walked along the beach, beyond the sight line of the house. I sat down on the sand, hugging my knees to my chest, and cried.

⁂

I didn't know the exact moment it happened. The sky was growing light when I saw him walking toward me on the beach.

"He didn't put up a fight," Renard said to me. "I wonder if he was expecting us?"

"I said nothing to him." I wiped away my tears.

"Yes, but perhaps he knew that you being here was too good to be true."

I angrily took off my right shoe and ripped out the insole. Beneath it was a GPS tracking chip. I flung it into the sea.

"We'll take you back to Papeete shortly," Renard said. "You can spend the day and night there. You must be exhausted. Your flight back to Paris leaves tomorrow morning."

I stared at the sea, trying to stifle my sobs.

Renard turned to leave and then looked back at me. "You did the right thing."

November 2015

LIZ

When I woke up the next day, a Friday, the story of Émile's capture was all over the news. Tahitian police, with Renard present, had found him at his beach bungalow at daybreak and arrested him.

That morning, Hobbs stopped by for coffee at my apartment and shared all the details. Kamal and I were riveted to his account of what had happened.

He told us that Sylvie, in a confrontation with her attorney, had confessed to knowing about the forgery. The attorney had persuaded her to negotiate a deal and called Renard, whose team took over. They told her to get in touch with Émile's contact and imbedded a GPS chip in her shoe, knowing that her handlers would likely trash her phone.

"Renard earned his pay this week." Hobbs chuckled. "Liz, remember that surveillance photo I showed you?"

I nodded. "She was almost unrecognizable."

"If it hadn't been for that chip, she could have easily disappeared."

"What will happen to her now? And Émile?" Kamal asked.

"She led the police to him. That was the deal. Charges won't be brought against her." Hobbs took a swig of his coffee. "If the original painting is recovered, there will be some legal wrangling. She still owes Sotheby's $6 million. But Émile is on the hook for conspiracy to commit forgery."

"And the guy who ran the forgery ring – what was his name?" I asked. "Has he been caught?"

Hobbs smiled. "Paul Durand. That's one of his names, at least. He's still at large. But if he's going to escape the Interpol's dragnet, he'll need to be a very artful dodger."

"So what about *Renée*, the painting that got away?" I felt such an attachment to her.

"It might take awhile to find her." Hobbs patted my hand. "You and I need to stay in touch, Sherlock. You know her almost as well as Bonnard himself."

―❦―

The weather had turned cold. As I was getting ready to run some errands later that morning, I put on my puffer jacket, but could barely get it zipped.

Kamal smiled. "I think the two of you need a new coat. Go buy yourself something warm and beautiful. My treat."

I happened to be near Printemps department store on Boulevard Haussmann that afternoon and decided to do a little shopping. I was surprised to be greeted by an armed security guard, who asked me to open my handbag as I entered the store. The new hyper-vigilance was so jarring to me at times. A painful reminder of a world gone crazy.

I rode the escalator to the second floor, enjoying the glittery Christmas decorations.

A friendly young saleswoman navigated me through the racks. I fell in love with a cashmere swing coat, with lots of growing room, in a lovely plum color that complemented my auburn hair.

I decided to wear the coat home. Kamal was delighted when I walked through the door. "Hello, gorgeous," he said, as he wrapped me in his arms and kissed me.

꠷

We had made dinner plans that night with Kamal's cousin Dev, who was visiting from Mumbai. We were to meet him at a popular restaurant in the 10th *arrondissement,* where he was staying with friends.

I was tired and secretly wanted to stay home. But I knew how much Kamal was looking forward to seeing him. This would be our only chance. Dev was leaving the next day.

We arrived at about eight. The restaurant was lively, with great music. Dev was a funny guy and full of stories. He and Kamal had grown up together, partners in mischief. I was in tears laughing at tales of their escapades. It was wonderful seeing Kamal enjoying himself so much.

The waiter had just served our dinners when firecrackers began popping outside.

Kamal glanced toward the front window. "What's that about?"

And then everything became a blur. Suddenly, the window shattered. The front door burst open. Three hooded gunmen, dressed in black, with automatic rifles, sprayed the room with bullets, yelling something I couldn't understand.

Kamal pushed me under the table. A split second later, he collapsed beside me, blood oozing from his chest, as the shooting continued.

"Kamal!"

"Shhh!" He covered my mouth. "Don't make a sound."

I could see he was losing consciousness. "Look at me, Kamal. Look at me!"

"Play dead," he whispered. His eyes closed.

Abruptly, the shooting stopped. Moans of pain filled the room. A woman sobbed. One of the gunmen shot off another round. And then the room went quiet.

I heard footsteps. From under the table, I saw steel-toed boots coming toward me. I tried to play dead, but I was breathing too hard. I opened my eyes to see a rifle pointed at me.

The young man holding the gun looked a lot like Tomar.

November 2015

SYLVIE

I ARRIVED BACK in Paris two days after the tragedy. I knew none of the victims. But I had seen the horrific photos and read about some of those who had been slain.

I went to a small restaurant in the 10th *arrondissement* where many had died. I laid a bouquet of flowers, among so many others, on the sidewalk there.

My own pain felt dwarfed by the grief and anguish that surrounded me.

I couldn't stop thinking of Émile and how I had sacrificed him in my own bout with madness.

November 2015

LIZ

MIRACULOUSLY, DEV, KAMAL and I survived the attack. Dev had only cuts and bruises. But Kamal's injuries were serious. He was in intensive care for days, following surgery to remove a bullet that had perforated a lung and lodged near his spine.

I had been taken to a different hospital. I had no wounds, but doctors feared the trauma might cause me to miscarry. I was kept under observation, with complete bed rest, for a week.

When I awoke at the hospital, the day after the attack, Asan was at my bedside praying. At first, I thought it all had been a horrible dream. "Tomar," I said to Asan. "I saw Tomar."

Asan laid his head on the bed and wept.

During my week in the hospital, Hobbs visited me every day. He told me a little bit about what the police knew, but didn't go into detail. Dev visited every day as well. He assured me Kamal's condition was stable.

But what he didn't tell me was that Kamal hadn't spoken since the shooting. Not a word.

On the day I was discharged, Dev came to take me home, but I insisted that we go see Kamal.

"Liz, let's see how you feel. Maybe tomorrow."

"No, Dev. Please. I want to see him now." I could tell by Dev's expression that something was wrong. "What is it? Is there something you haven't told me?"

"Kamal has lost his ability to speak."

"What?"

"The doctors say it's psychological trauma. There's no physical injury to explain it."

We went straight to the hospital. Kamal was asleep when Dev and I entered the room. He was surrounded by IV poles and beeping monitors. A massive bandage was taped to his chest.

I stood beside the bed and held his hand. He opened his eyes and looked at me.

"I'm here, Kamal. I'm here." I gently placed his hand on my belly. "We're fine."

Tears streamed down his cheeks. His mouth moved slightly. But no words came.

April 2016

LIZ

DURING THE WEEKS and months after the November 13 attacks in Paris, I swung between gratitude and despair.

It was indeed Tomar standing over me that night. In his last act of kindness in this world, he spared me. But moments later, he blew himself up. Grief-stricken Asan saddled himself with blame.

I thought a lot about fate and karma and the path Kamal and I had taken after our wheels locked at Charles de Gaulle on that rainy July morning.

Had we invited the bad karma that rained down on us as we recklessly began an affair that would end his marriage and take his son away from him? Kamal forever would be haunted by a heart-wrenching *what if* – would his son still be alive if he had stayed in his marriage?

I knew there was no easy road back from this dark place. But every day, I put my feet on the floor with hope and intention as I helped Kamal in his recovery. Despite all that had happened, I still felt a ray of light was within sight. We had a baby on the way – a little girl, we learned, who would be born in May.

When Kamal was well enough to travel, we went back to London. His doctors there had no concrete explanation for his speech loss, but they were cautiously optimistic. His therapist urged me not to lose hope. "Patience, patience," he'd say to me. "Keep loving him and encouraging him."

Loving was the easy part. But patience was not so easy for me. I desperately wanted Kamal back, all of him. He had healed from his physical wounds. I was so thankful for that. He was learning to talk to me with his hands, as he caressed my face or turned the corners of my mouth into a smile. He had become adept at scribbling messages on a pad he carried with him.

But I longed for the sound of his voice. Sometimes I lay awake at night as he slept beside me, remembering how he used to say my name, the way he'd whisper *my darling* as we made love. I didn't want to forget.

I thought about Sylvie and what she had lost. Surely she had loved Émile once. And by all accounts, he loved her and did all he could to have a life with her in his exile. What if they had been content to sell her grandfather's Bonnard and live happily on the proceeds that would have given them a very comfortable life together? But greed had gotten the better of them.

And Bonnard himself – I couldn't help but see him as a selfish bastard who had caused the tragedy in his life. Bedding the lovely Renée, half his age, romancing her in Rome and leading her to believe he would marry her. And then, in a capricious change of heart, he married Marthe, his tormented loyal mistress. An action, born of guilt or pity, that would cause a beautiful despairing young woman to end her life.

In those dark days, I kept groping toward the light.

And then one day, another miracle happened. Kamal woke up and kissed me, as was his way each morning. "I love you," he said. Just like that.

For a moment, we were too shocked for words. And then, the tenderest words of love and gratitude came tumbling out of both us.

Author's Epilogue

The idea for this book came to me one divine spring afternoon, in May 2015, as I sat in the garden of the house that once had belonged to Pierre Bonnard. The property sits on the Seine, in Vernonnet, France, just a few kilometers from Giverny, where Bonnard's friend Claude Monet lived for many years.

I've always loved Bonnard's exquisite garden scenes, and there I was that day in the very place he had painted some of them. From my garden bench, I looked up at the house, which he called Ma Roulotte – my caravan – a modest, two-story, brick-and-stucco structure with a white balcony railing, in a crosshatch design, that appeared in some of his paintings.

The upstairs room that opens onto the balcony had been his studio, where he'd tack unstretched canvases to the wall as he worked on them. He typically painted from memory, referring to sketches he had made in his daybook, in which he routinely noted the weather along with the colors and scenes that presented during his morning walks. His canvases were works-in-progress for years, as he added daubs of paint that he carefully mixed with the skill of an alchemist. According to Bonnard lore, he once asked his close friend and fellow artist Édouard Vuillard to distract a museum guard while he touched up one of his paintings on display.

The present owners of the Bonnard house are Danièle Teisseire and Bertrand de Vautibault, who meticulously have staged the main rooms in the style of Bonnard, based on his photos and paintings. Danièle and Bertrand welcome visitors, by appointment. "This is not a house that we should keep to ourselves," Danièle says. "We must share it."

The upstairs room that had been Bonnard's studio is now the living area and looks out over the garden, with a view of the Seine. On the day of my first visit, Danièle served juice and Madeleines at a table by the balcony. A vase with a bouquet of cabbagey apricot roses sat next to a stack of Bonnard art books.

Downstairs, a room that had been part of Bonnard's living area is now a bedroom. His painting *Dining Room in the Country* shows Marthe standing outside the house, leaning in through the open window of that room. Danièle imitated Marthe's pose, much to my delight.

I am very grateful to Danièle and Bertrand for sharing their home with me, along with their stories of the man who owned it from 1912 to 1939. I'd also like to thank Vernon resident and artist Marie-Noëlle Révérend for her friendship and assistance as a translator during my research visits.

There's no definitive biography about Bonnard and often the details of his personal life are as sketchy as his daybook jottings. Dates and facts conflict. His correspondence with close friends reveals little about his emotional state, though it was clear in his later years with Marthe that he felt the walls closing in.

In one letter, dated 1932, he wrote: "Poor Marthe has become completely misanthropic. She no longer wants to see anyone, not even her old friends, and we are condemned to absolute solitude."

On the day she died in 1942, Bonnard noted in his daybook there was a blustery Mistral – the fierce wind that often buffets southern France, where he and Marthe were living at the time – and he drew a simple cross denoting his wife's passing. That was all.

I felt great empathy for Marthe and Renée as I pieced together their stories. Clearly, Bonnard loved Marthe. His early bedroom nudes of her were imbued with a lover's tenderness and desire. But as her problems overtook them both, he painted her with detachment, as a dispassionate observer of her most private moments. In some of his paintings, she seems to disappear into the picture.

Renée was born in 1900 and was in her late teens – somewhere between 16 and 18 – when she met Bonnard, who asked her to model for him. It seems she was friendly with Marthe initially, and in fact, she stayed with Bonnard and Marthe at their home in Vernonnet.

It's unclear exactly when Bonnard and Renée became lovers. In 1921, he took her to Rome. He met with her parents to ask their permission to marry her. He was in his 50s then, no doubt exhilarated by the rush of having an attractive young lover and by the possibility of escaping his oppressive life with Marthe.

Before Bonnard met Renée, he'd had a short-lived fling with a woman named Lucienne Dupuy de Frenelle, whom he painted. During Bonnard's dalliances, fragile Marthe hung on. But she came undone when Bonnard told her he planned to marry Renée. A few weeks after he wed Marthe, Renée committed suicide. Details differ about how and where she died. Some sources say she shot herself. According to other accounts, she drowned in a bathtub.

On my second visit to the house in Vernonnet, in April 2016, I looked at the setting differently, imaging Marthe and Renée in close quarters there, as rivals for Bonnard's attention and affection.

Quite likely, Bonnard painted *Young Women in the Garden* at the house in Vernonnet. He began the painting in the early 1920s and hid it from Marthe following their marriage in 1925, despite her demands that he destroy his renderings of Renée. After Marthe's death, he re-worked the canvas, infusing it with a golden backdrop, as if creating a halo around his beloved young mistress. Many accounts refer to Renée as a blonde, but some art historians say that Bonnard lightened her hair posthumously. Her hair is reddish brown in *Portrait de femme (Renée Monchaty)* c. 1920, which had been in the collection of his great-nephew Antoine Terrasse before it was put up for auction in 2015.

In my research, I read many articles by art historians and critics and tried to balance varying opinions and observations. One especially informative source for me was a book entitled *The Accidental Masterpiece: On the Art of Life and Vice Versa* by Michael Kimmelman, who devoted a chapter to the story of Marthe and Renée.

I wish to thank Philip Samuel Sundqvist and Julio Nicacio for giving this book a cover that, in keeping with the story, presents a slightly altered Bonnard. (Discerning eyes will note the cover image, inspired by Bonnard's *Nu dans un intérieur*, is not an exact copy of the artist's original.) I'd also like to thank graphic designer Elizabeth MacFarland for her artistry.

The painting *Renée* is fictional – though, as Liz would say, it's so *plausible*. The modern-day layer of this story and its characters, including Bonnard's gardener, are my invention, as is Émile's account of the forgeries at the Uffizi Gallery in Florence.

That said, there is a man whose luggage cart snared mine at Charles de Gaulle Airport some years ago. What followed could be the opening of a book, I thought at the time. I must confess he had lovely hazel eyes.

And with that, I'll leave you with a wink.

Made in the USA
Lexington, KY
18 May 2017